Long Past Dawn Copyright © 2023 Lorhainne Ekelund

Editor: Talia Leduc
All rights reserved.
ISBN-13: 978-1998775675

Give feedback on the book at:
lorhainneeckhart@hotmail.com

Twitter: @LEckhart
Facebook: AuthorLorhainneEckhart

Printed in the U.S.A

Long Past Dawn

THE FRIESSENS
BOOK THIRTY

LORHAINNE ECKHART

The Friessen Family Series
Reading order:

The Outsider Series

The Forgotten Child
A Baby And A Wedding
Fallen Hero
The Awakening
Secrets
Runaway
Overdue
The Unexpected Storm
The Wedding

The Friessens: A New Beginning

The Deadline
The Price to Love
A Different Kind of Love
A Vow of Love, A Friessen Family Christmas

The Friessens

The Reunion
The Bloodline
The Promise
The Business Plan
The Decision
First Love
Family First
Leave the Light On
In the Moment
In the Family: A Friessen Family Christmas
In the Silence
In the Stars
In the Charm
Unexpected Consequences
It Was Always You
The First Time I Saw You
Welcome to My Arms
Welcome to Boston (A Paige & Morgan Short Story)
I'll Always Love You
Ground Rules
A Reason to Breathe
You Are My Everything
Anything For You
The Homecoming includes When They Were Young
Stay Away From My Daughter
The Bad Boy
A Place of Our Own
The Visitor
All About Devon
Long Past Dawn
How to Heal a Heart
Keep Me In Your Heart

The Friessen Family

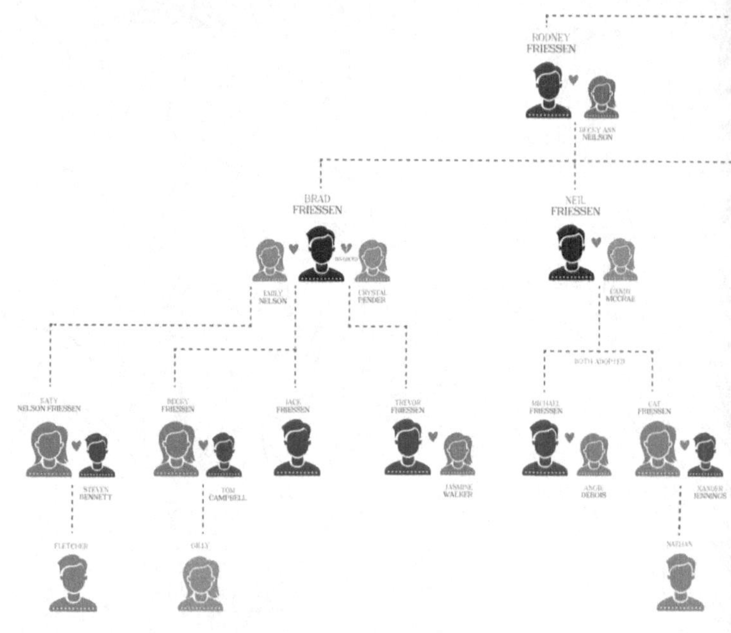

The Outsider Series

THE FORGOTTEN CHILD	BRAD & EMILY
A BABY AND A WEDDING	BRAD & EMILY & and Jed had Andrea & Becky
FALLEN HERO	JED, DIANA & ANDY
THE SEARCH	JED, DIANA & ANDY
THE AWAKENING	ANDY & LAURA

The Outsider Series

SECRETS	DIANA & JED with the entire Friessen Family
RUNAWAY	ANDY & LAURA
OVERDUE	JED & DIANA
THE UNEXPECTED STORM	NEIL & CANDY
THE WEDDING	NEIL & CANDY and the entire Friessen Family

The Friessens: A New Beginning

THE DEADLINE	ANDY & LAURA
THE PRICE TO LOVE	NEIL & CANDY
A DIFFERENT KIND OF LOVE	BRAD & EMILY
A VOW OF LOVE	THE ENTIRE
A FRIESSEN FAMILY CHRISTMAS	FRIESSEN FAMILY

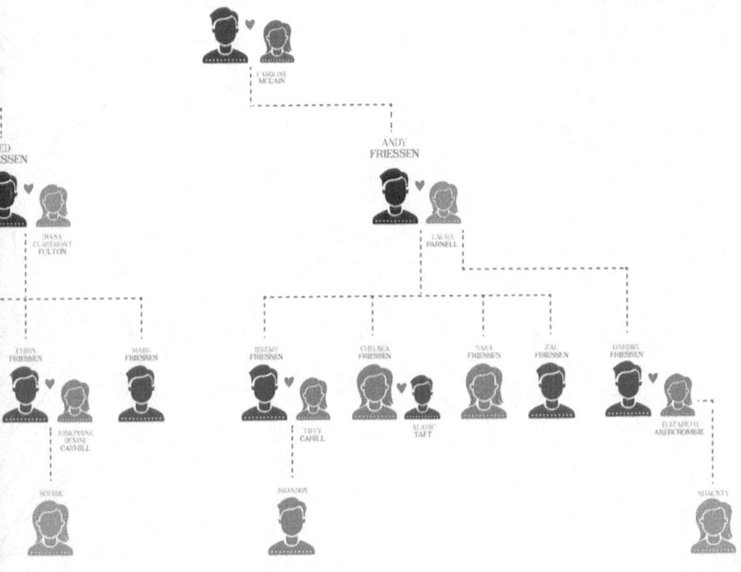

The Friessens

THE ENTIRE FRIESSEN FAMILY	
ANDY & LAURA	
JED & DIANA	
NEIL & CANDY	
BRAD & EMILY	
KATY & STEVEN	
KATY & STEVEN	

The Friessens

LEAVE THE LIGHT ON	KATY & STEVEN
IN THE MOMENT	BECKY & TOM
IN THE FAMILY	THE ENTIRE FRIESSEN FAMILY
IN THE SILENCE	CAT & XANDER
IN THE STARS	DANNY & EVIE
IN THE CHARM	CHRIS & J.D.
UNEXPECTED CONSEQUENCES	CHRIS & J.D.

The Friessens

IT WAS ALWAYS YOU	KATY & STEVEN
THE FIRST TIME I SAW YOU	GABRIEL & ELIZABETH
WELCOME TO MY ARMS	CHELSEA & ALARIC
WELCOME TO BOSTON	PAIGE & MORGAN
I'LL ALWAYS LOVE YOU	JEREMY
GROUND RULES	JEREMY & TIFFY
A REASON TO BREATHE	TREVOR & JASMINE
YOU ARE MY EVERYTHING	MICHAEL & ANGIE
ANYTHING FOR YOU	
THE HOMECOMING	THE ENTIRE FRIESSEN FAMILY

Long Past Dawn

Two years ago, Sara Friessen's life was changed forever when a young man from the wrong side of the tracks saved her from a brutal assault. To her, he is brilliant, her savior, the man she plans to marry and spend her life with, the only man she has ever given a piece of her heart.

But to Devon Reed, Sara is the girl he shouldn't love. No matter how much he tries, Devon, now a young law student, believes he isn't the kind of guy who should be with the daughter of Andy Friessen.

As he sets out to find justice for a mother who abandoned him when he was a child, struggling to undo a wrong and set the record straight, his life begins to unravel, and he finds more questions than answers. The ultimate cost could be his relationship with Sara, the love they have, and the future they planned together, which seems to be slipping away.

CHAPTER
One

Devon was late again.

Sara stared at her cell phone and the third text she'd sent, which he had yet to answer. "Glad that I rate so highly, Devon," she muttered and tossed her phone onto the counter between the fridge and stove.

She heard a key in the door and lifted her gaze from where she stood in the dated galley kitchen, both hopeful and angry at having been taken for granted. She took in the overcooked porkchops in the skillet on the older yellow stove and the pot of potatoes she knew were only lukewarm, thinking of the salad she hadn't bothered to make.

"Devon, it's after seven, and I'd appreciate…" She stopped talking. It was Anton, Devon's brother, wearing a bulky black hoodie, perpetually pissed off. Her heart sank.

"Sorry, babe, just me," he said. "So that answers my question. Guess Devon isn't home." He pocketed his keys as he swaggered in, and she had to remind herself why she needed to be civil to him.

"I'm not your babe, Anton. I have a name. I'm your brother's girlfriend. Some respect would be nice."

He didn't bother to look her way as he brushed past her to the dated fridge, also godawful yellow but a different shade than the stove, and reached in to grab a beer. He twisted off the cap and tossed it into the sink, where it landed in a cup with a clang. There it was, the disrespect again, considering she was the only one who cleaned this older two-bedroom apartment.

"Point taken," was all he said. Yup, he still didn't like her, but then, the feeling was mutual.

She just stared at his back as he strode to the sofa, lifted the remote to the large TV, which took up a good portion of the tiny apartment, and belched. He lowered his large frame and made himself comfortable.

"That dinner you made smells good," he said.

She rested a cookie sheet over the chops to try to keep them warm, and she again had to remind herself to answer Devon's brother politely. She wished he'd take the hint and move out instead of continuing to make her feel as if she were the interloper, the one who didn't belong.

"Yup, help yourself," she said, taking in the pot of mashed potatoes, as well, and the green beans in the oven. Last she'd looked, they were wilted and overdone.

"Don't mind if I do," he said, bumping past her, and she had to press her hand to the counter as he reached above her head to the cupboard and pulled out a plate for himself.

She stepped out of the kitchen. The dated dining

table was now free of its usual clutter—cards, keys, cartons, junk, everything that seemed to be dumped there instead of put away. Anton was pulling the green beans from the oven and dishing up a heaping plate, forking not two but three porkchops, then seemed to hesitate.

"Ah, there's only two left…" He gestured with his fork, and she just lifted her hand, surprised he'd bothered to ask.

"Take them, it's fine," she replied. "As you said, Devon's not here. If he can't at least give me a call and a heads-up that he's going to be late, then he can't expect me to keep dinner warm. Soon it'll be completely inedible, unless overcooked and tasteless is your thing…"

She realized Anton wasn't even listening. He grabbed a second beer and headed back to the living room, to his spot in the middle of the sofa, where he lifted the remote and turned on some epic videogame battle.

"Then stop cooking for him," he said. "Seriously, although it works for me, I can't believe you're in there, cooking. He's busy, you know, being a law student, interning, and trying to make a difference. His head's elsewhere, you know, with more important things. It's as if you expect him to do a nine to five and then come home to you. It's not all about you there, babe. You can't expect him to drop everything—"

"And come home for dinner because he said he would? You mean I can't expect him to keep his word and actually show up, because that's what you do when you're in a relationship? I said I was cooking dinner, and he said yes, he'd be here."

Anton shoved the potatoes and beans in his mouth around a hunk of porkchop. He was shaking his head and jabbed his knife her way. "You know what, Sara? I'm tired of hearing you complain about it. If you don't like his hours, then leave."

Was he serious? She pulled her arms over her chest, taking a second to push up the sleeves of her dark blue T-shirt. Her feet were in socks, and her jeans hung low and loose on her hips. She fisted her hands, reminding herself again that Anton was Devon's only brother.

"You want me to move out?" she stated.

This time, he froze with the fork to his mouth before shoveling in more of the dinner she had cooked, and he pulled his dark gaze from the TV over to her, allowing it to scrape down her body before landing on her feet. She hated when he did that. That one look told her what he really thought of who she was.

"That's totally your choice. Far be it from me to tell you what to do. But then think of how we'd miss doing this, me listening to you complain and such. Yeah, I imagine the peace and quiet may be kind of overwhelming, and I wouldn't have to deal with all those girly products in my bathroom. Let me think about that." He paused for a second, and she was too stunned at his arrogance to say anything. "Hell, yeah! Please leave."

She pressed her lips together and nodded, gripping her arms. "You know what? I have a better idea. Since I'm Devon's girlfriend and he's the one who wants me here with him, and there are two of us and only one of you, how about you move out?" She circled her finger toward the door.

He laughed as he scooped up another huge forkful

and shoved it in his mouth. "Nope, this is my place, and in case you forgot, my name's on the lease," he said as he chewed. Sometimes Anton's manners rivalled that of a barn animal. She watched him slice a huge piece of pork, look at it, and then drag his gaze back over to her. "Sounds to me as if you're trying to come between me and Devon."

The way he said it had her walking back into the galley kitchen and taking in the mess from dinner, then walking right back out again. "No, Anton, I just want some respect. I think I deserve it, and seriously, you think I don't know you don't like me and have no use for me? You make your point every day, but you know what? I live here too, and I don't want to watch you taking over the living room and the TV every night with your video games. Shut it down now, and for that matter, since I do all the cooking here and you seem to have no problem eating everything I cook, you can clean up. I'm not your maid, yet I'm the only one picking up things, vacuuming, cleaning, washing the floors. I swear, before I moved in, I don't think you and Devon ever cleaned."

She didn't think she'd ever seen shock on his face. Then he started laughing. "Hey, there should be some benefit to having you here…"

"You chauvinistic a-hole…" she growled, hearing a key in the door but not turning to it, fighting the urge to wrap her hands around Anton's thick neck and squeeze. But she couldn't do that.

He was laughing again, her food still in his mouth. "A-hole? Is that the best you've got?"

She was already walking over to the TV. He had the

remote on the sofa beside him, so she reached around and pulled the cord from the wall to unplug it. His expression was priceless, and she was still holding the cord as Devon walked in, wearing a white dress shirt and navy suit, his tie pulled loose, a second-hand briefcase tucked under his arm.

His heavy gaze landed on her and the cord. "And what's going on here?" he said.

"I can't believe you did that, you fucking little troublemaker!" Anton snapped, not pulling his gaze from her. Mad was mad, and Anton had a way of looking at her when he was angry that would've made a sane person think twice about provoking him.

"Hey!" Devon shouted, turning to his brother. "Don't you dare talk to my girl like that—and you, what the hell are you doing?" He was already walking toward her, his hand out as he gestured to the cord.

She dropped it to the floor and stepped away. "Trying for a little peace around here. Seriously, Devon, your brother's on that TV the minute he walks through the door. Just this morning, Mr. Lewis from 7B commented on the noise from video games until all hours. It's waking him up and keeping him awake."

He hadn't, really. In fact, when she'd brought it up, he'd said it wasn't really a big deal. She felt her cheeks warm, and she stepped around Devon into the kitchen when he didn't touch her. She didn't hear what he said to his brother, but the next thing she heard was Anton's footsteps and the door to his bedroom closing.

Devon appeared in the doorway to the kitchen as she took in what should have been dinner. "Do you think you could try to get along with my brother?" he said, his hand on the frame of the door. She didn't miss the way he stared down at the potatoes in the pot, the wilted green beans, and the two dry porkchops in the frying pan. Everything was cold.

"I've tried, Devon, but it's not all on me. He doesn't want me here and makes no secret of it, the way he talks to me, treats me, and…"

He was right in her space, his hands on her arms. "I want you here. What Anton wants doesn't enter into the equation. It's you and me, remember?"

He leaned down and kissed her, and she went on her tiptoes, feeling his hands slide around her and over her ass, pulling her closer. She tasted his coffee, his day, and she pulled back, still in his arms. He took in dinner on the stove.

"It's cold, you know," she said.

He pulled in a breath, "Sorry, something came up."

Something always came up. This time, when his brooding gaze fell on her, she saw that something hadn't gone right. Devon didn't share everything. No, scratch that. He was as closed off as every male she'd ever known—her father, her brothers. Then there was his mother's case, which she knew had taken up his entire focus and made him change course, studying to become a lawyer.

He said nothing more as he stepped back, reached into the frying pan, and lifted a porkchop to take a bite. She knew she'd have to wait all day for him to say something. He was a man stuck in his head.

"It's fine," he said. "Thanks for cooking."

She blinked, realizing he was talking about the dinner, which she'd wanted to be special. He took another bite before dropping the chop back in the frying pan and reaching for a towel hanging by the sink to wipe his hands.

"It's not fine," she said. "So how about you tell me about your day and what's really going on? I can always tell by that look. Is it your mom's case or something else?"

There it was, the pull of his lips that hinted at a smile. He gave her all of his hard gaze, and just the way he looked at her, she felt as if he could see everything, even the things she showed no one, the private, personal side of herself that she didn't let others have. She also knew she was one of the few people that Devon, who wrote the book on being closed off, actually let in.

"Shows, huh?" He shook his head, and she waited. "It was just one of those days, those shitty days where all the work I've done appears to be a waste of time. The piles of casework, paperwork, filings…and you know what I did for the last two hours of my day?"

She just stared at him with a sick feeling in her stomach. She knew how hard he worked. She shook her head.

"I packed up the files, put everything in boxes, and carried it all to the storage room, where it'll go with all the other closed cases. My boss said it was dead in the water, no more appeals, and the parole board isn't going to hear her now. I was told they have no more time to put into my mother's case."

She didn't know what to say, fearing saying the wrong thing. "So now what?"

Devon shrugged, pushed away from the counter, and stepped around her, not touching her although she was so close. "I'm going to take a shower and then hit the books."

That was it. She stared in shock at his back as he walked out of the kitchen, and she listened to the bathroom door close, feeling completely shut out and at a loss of what to say. This was the one thing she'd never expected from Devon, for him to simply give up and walk away.

CHAPTER
Two

How many times had he seen his mother in the past two years? He'd lost count, between visiting days and meetings with the lawyers. Each time, she transformed little by little from a stranger, filled with sorrow and fear, her familiar expression so much like Anton's, to his mother, whose expression was one of hope.

When had the anger he'd held toward her for so long diminished? Maybe it was him who had let go after seeing the vulnerability she didn't try to hide, the tears she'd shed in embarrassment. The lawyers had offered her some optimism.

He allowed the hot water to run over his back and head as he pressed a hand against the wall of the shower, trying to will away what he had to do, which was tell his mother she would never get out until she did the one thing she refused to do again: lie.

He heard the door and pulled the shower curtain open, seeing Sara lifting her shirt over her head and tossing it on the heap of the vanity with his dress clothes, which needed a trip to the cleaners.

"What are you doing?" he said, taking in her confident, determined expression as she reached behind herself and unhooked her bra. She gave it a toss as she stepped out of the rest of her clothes, and he took in her incredible body, her full breasts, creamy white skin, and long legs. She stepped into the tub shower, suddenly crammed full with both of them.

"You have to ask, Devon?" she said. "It seems if I let you slither off, you'll wallow and shut down and pull into yourself, and we won't speak for days. So here I am." She turned around, and her long blond hair hung halfway down her back in soft waves. He loved everything about her. "Wash my back," she said and glanced over her shoulder, waiting, determined.

He reached for the soap in the shower caddy and lathered it in his hands before pressing them over her shoulders, her back. She lifted her hair. It wasn't lost on him, the contrast from his hands to her soft and creamy skin, which was perfect and familiar and his.

"That feels good," she said. "So what happened with the case? I know you've spent so long on this, the appeals, the parole board hearings…"

He thought about the rest, too, about how he'd been trying to get her ex-boyfriend, Darnell, who'd talked her into taking the fall for him, to finally come clean. It would mean everything and would go a long way toward explaining why she'd done what she'd done.

"You know a chance of parole will never happen for her," he said. "She's now trying to do the right thing, but she's already confessed."

He'd finally seen the video, the one the cops had made to cover their asses and ensure there'd be no questions about her confession. It had sealed her fate and was the nail in her coffin. She'd been so convincing, and he knew she'd been high, but that was the image of the woman he'd always remembered, the woman he'd hated. Watching it had brought back that day so many years earlier when a mother wrapped up in her own misery did the stupidest thing a woman could do: take the fall for a guy without even a thought as to what would happen to her children.

Sara turned in the shower, stepping closer to him, body to body, skin to skin, the water running over her, too. Her hands ran over his chest, feeling his pecs, his abs. It was a familiar touch that he welcomed, and her all-knowing green eyes didn't shy away. She gave him all of herself, never filling an awkward silence with talk or using words to try to make something better.

"Turn around," she said. "I'll wash your back, too." She gestured and reached for the soap, and he did as instructed, shutting his eyes as he put his face in the spray. Now what was he going to do? The question ran through his head over and over, even though her touch was a welcome distraction.

"So how come you're not trying to make me feel better, or telling me to get off my ass and get out there and try something else, or saying I did my best?" he said. That was what Anton would say. His brother expected a miracle where their mom was concerned. Devon wasn't ready to face him, because he already knew he wouldn't take it well.

Her hands ran over his back along with the warm,

welcoming water, and she leaned in and pressed a kiss to his shoulder as she slid her arms around him, and he felt all her softness pressing into him.

He could've turned around then and pressed her against the wet tile. He pictured her legs around his waist as he tried to ease some of his misery. She'd have let him, too. He'd feel better in the moment, and then he wouldn't. He didn't move as she rocked against him, her hand touching him, running over his stomach and lower, taking hold of him. He hissed and then sucked in a breath and groaned.

"You really want me to use words, tell you how amazing you are to prop up your ego? Maybe you want me to say I know you did your best, and no one could have done more than you, or it's okay to give up, it's okay to cut your losses and move on. Why would I say that, Devon? You're the last person who needs anyone, especially me, to remind you that you've done your best and it's good enough. You do nothing halfway. I know what you've put into your mom's case. I know what it's taken from you. I know you've searched every nook to find anything that would get your mom out.

"You've worked all-nighters alongside her lawyers and then went out the door to school at dawn, looking for some legal precedent, some piece of evidence, anything. So if you want me to say not to beat yourself up, fine, I'll say it. But I really think you don't need to hear it from me, because I know you've done more than any person could or would do. You've gone beyond the impossible because that's who you are. So no, I'm not going to add my voice or try to make you feel better. I'm going to just be here and maybe wallow with you."

As he listened to the spray of water and felt the heat, her warmth, he still didn't turn around. Her hand ran over his chest and back, over his pecs, his stomach, just touching, feeling, being there. She didn't push, knowing there were some things he just couldn't share about the case. She never tried to pry it from him. He'd never met anyone with the principles this girl had.

"He said no," Devon finally said.

Her hands stilled, but she didn't pull away. He felt her cheek press to his back. "Who?"

"Darnell, the boyfriend she took the fall for, the one who talked her into saying the guns were hers. He said all the right things, like she'd get only a year or two, but he'd get life because of the three-strike law. In fact, that law came down on Mom. She got it, and he let her rot, never once tried to see her. You know that already. He never answered her letters because he moved on to another woman and continued his life of crime—more guns, more drugs. The cops knew. Her first lawyer left a note in the file. Of course, they had their eyes on him, and the next woman wouldn't take the fall for him. She was smarter. He's in the federal pen, doing life, so what would coming clean mean for him and his sentence?"

He turned around and took in the caring, the support, the love in her eyes as she looked up at him. Her hair was damp and hanging loose. He couldn't picture his life without this woman. He loved Sara so much.

"Apparently not what you hoped," she said.

She wasn't a ditzy blonde. He didn't know why the thought hit him now. It was a joke between them. He wondered what fool had coined that term.

He just shook his head. "Nope. Word came down from the prison. All our requests to see him were denied. He's not interested in talking, said he doesn't remember who she is."

CHAPTER

Three

S he took in the construction site, the oversized bin that took up all of the driveway, and the house with tacky blue siding. Her brother's tan pickup and the electrician's van were the only vehicles parked out front in a subdivision not far from downtown.

She stepped out of her black pickup, the one her father had given her years earlier, for which she hadn't paid one dime. It was comfortable. She hadn't had any of the struggles Devon had while growing up. At times, being with him, she was reminded of how lucky she was. She couldn't imagine wanting him any other way, because everything he had come through and survived had made him the man she loved today.

She pulled in a breath, trekking into the slush of melting snow. She could feel the morning chill through her faded blue jeans even with her navy down coat. Her hands were bare, and she could still feel Devon's touch on her, as well as the weariness from the hours she'd lain awake beside him while he snored softly. At least one good thing had come from the after-shower sex in bed, damp and needy, a tender taking—just her and him in his cramped room, which barely fit a double bed, touching her, loving her, and saying everything of what she meant to him without words. He'd been asleep as soon as he rolled off her.

Now, her heart ached for his mother, whom she'd met only once.

"Hey, it's about time you got here," Gabriel called out. "The revised plans came in last night. Did you have a chance to look at them?" He pulled on a black toque as he stepped out from behind the bin. His three-day beard was now turning four. She hadn't seen him. She'd been lost in thought.

"No, didn't get a chance to check my email yet. Came straight here." She clutched the strap of her over-sized bag, into which she'd tucked her small laptop, and started up the driveway, seeing the mud and debris, knowing the house had been taken back to the studs inside. "I see the electrician finally showed. Does that mean progress is being made?"

What design changes had the architect sent this time? She wondered how many more times she'd have to send it back. It was just one of those things. Some houses came together easier than others. This project had been a nightmare from day one, with all kinds of hidden finds.

"To a certain extent, yeah," Gabriel said. "As long as we can get everyone on board with the changes, namely you, we should be good. He's wiring downstairs, putting in the new electrical box to cover all the upgrades."

Her brother was already walking into the house, and banging echoed in the open space. A man swore, and she scanned the cords, generator, and power tools that were part of all her brother's builds.

"So, in case I didn't say it, Sara," he continued, "look it over, approve it, and don't be difficult this time, or this brother–sister team will have the shortest operation record in the general contracting business."

She didn't have to look up from her laptop on the worktable beside the chop saw to know her brother was stressed again. She spotted the email with the PDF attachment and opened it, taking in the floor plan, the changes made, and the notes before looking back over to Gabriel, who was standing at one of the new windows, looking out at a backyard that was simply a mud pit. She knew what he was waiting for.

"I see the beam is still there—two of them, to be exact, which kills the open concept we were after…"

"The open concept *you* were after. Let's be clear about that. I maintained from day one that what we find when we take walls out dictates how open the concept can be."

Yup, he was stressed. She had to suck in another breath as she stared at the drawings, trying to figure out whether she could live with her name on the changes she was seeing. "It seems every day I show up here, there are more changes. Sometimes I really hate surprises. It would be great if just once, everything would go the way it was supposed to, easy, with no hurdles, not making everything so damn hard."

"Sounds to me as if we're not talking about the changes. Something else going on?"

She rested her hand on the laptop as she lifted her gaze to Gabriel, who was still wearing his knit winter hat. She could see his breath in the chill of the room.

Her hands were cold, so she shoved them in her jacket pockets.

"Do you regret the day you asked me to join you in this business, when you decided to stop working for everyone else and start doing your own homebuilding and renovation?"

He didn't smile. Something had been off about her brother as of late, and she wondered what was on his mind. Was it Elizabeth, Shaunty, something else? Gabriel was just like Jeremy, just like her dad, just like Devon. She wondered if it would kill any of them to share something of how they were feeling.

"Sure," he said. "When I saw your drawings, some of the ideas you had were better than the professionals I worked with. You're a natural at what you do—or are you trying to say this isn't for you?"

She could see he was in that place, the dark one she couldn't remember him having been in for a long time. Doom and gloom, or was he looking to end their partnership of six months? "No, Gabriel, don't start reading into what I'm saying. I love this job, and believe it or not, even though we butt heads with these changes you go ahead and make without talking to me, I still love working with you. There are days you test my patience, though."

At least that brought the hint of a smile to his lips. "Oops," he said. "So what did Devon do?"

She closed the laptop. How did he know? "It's not what he did," she said. "He's been working so long on his mom's case, for almost two years. He changed his major and started law school, and he's worked his ass off, helping the lawyers on his mom's case to offset the cost. I've watched him and supported him from the sidelines. Every draft he's written, all the cases he's studied, all the files he's read…it's just mind boggling, the detail. Not a job I could do, but he's been on it.

"Last night, he came home and said it was over, done, lost. He was told to pack everything up, all the case files, because she's never going to get out. You know how his mother confessed to something she didn't do? Well, the parole hearings require her to show remorse, except she's now refusing to lie. It's quite a mess, really. Devon has tried to get in touch with her ex-boyfriend, who's in for life. It wouldn't hurt him to tell the truth, to do the right thing. It's not as if he can get any more time. But apparently he says he doesn't even remember who she is."

She took in the shock on her brother's face as he shook his head. "Yeah, that's exactly how I feel. Like, how do you not remember destroying someone's life?" She lifted her hands, then tucked them back in her pockets, feeling the chill and not knowing what else to say. This Saturday, would Devon drive to the prison to see his mother? She'd been along with him only the one time. Devon had refused to let her come again.

"I don't know what to say, Sara," Gabriel replied. "Sometimes, life isn't fair. Sometimes, doing the right thing at the wrong time can actually work against you."

The way he said it, she thought there was more, but she heard a knock on the wood framing and turned to see her dad standing there, just inside the door, beside the beam that was their source of contention. He wore a black bomber jacket, and his icy blue eyes took her in. She'd always felt as if she could do anything, be anything, because of her dad.

"Hi, Dad. Didn't know you were coming by," Gabriel said.

Andy looked around at the space where the living room would be and where she was standing, which was where the island in the kitchen would go. "Thought I would stop in and see how my investment is doing," he replied. His shrewd gaze never missed a thing. It was just who he was. He was also the money behind Friessen Quality Construction, a silent investor who always added an opinion.

"Just waiting for Sara to sign off on the changes," Gabriel added, and she stared her brother's way, lifting a brow.

"Actually, I just wanted to point out to Gabriel the importance of teamwork," Sara said, "of staying on the same page, and of compromise. The posts have to go, Gabriel, as it will kill the flow. We want buyers to walk in and have that wow factor, not just to say, 'Okay, this is nice, but these two posts are taking from my sightlines.' Take those two posts out, and then it's a go. That's what we originally talked about."

Gabriel was shaking his head. "We're already fifteen over budget, Sara. The electrical problems kind of blew our contingency. If we want to make a profit, the posts stay. Otherwise, you can compromise by downgrading some of the finishes."

"You mean by cutting corners."

Gabriel only shrugged.

Andy walked into the middle of the space and was looking out the big windows that filled what would be the living room, from floor to ceiling. It would be a great view, letting in lots of light. She wondered why he was really there.

"No, I mean dialing it back," Gabriel said. "You want the posts gone, fine. That's about twelve to fifteen thousand in additional costs. We'll need to cut back on the appliances, change the granite countertop to laminate, and take the high-end finishes out of there. We can't keep everything or we'll just break even. Give or take, Sara. We need to make money here."

She thought for sure her dad would step in and say something, but he appeared distracted. That too was likely a ruse, though. He was always paying attention. He just had a way about him that fooled everyone.

She was tempted to lift the screen of her laptop, but she knew the changes Gabriel had made, and she knew what he was saying. She took in the posts that could ruin everything of what she wanted this house to be. This time, when she looked up, she realized her dad was watching her.

"Fine, I'll make cuts somewhere else," she said. "Just get rid of the posts, and I'll figure out where to take it out of."

"That wasn't so hard, was it?" Andy said, and for a minute, she thought he was teasing.

"Well, it would be easier if everything went according to plan," she replied, taking in Gabriel, who lifted his brows.

Her dad shook his head. "Life never works that way, Sara. Hate to tell you that. You can't control the outcome or some of the things that crop up, but what you can do is compromise like you did here. So the public defender is closing Tiera Reed's case."

She nodded. "You heard me just now, then."

Her dad inclined his head. "I didn't push with Devon. I gave him my lawyer's name, and I thought she was working on it. Wasn't sure why he went with a public defender. Not sure that was the wisest course."

What could she say to her dad without betraying Devon? She knew how he felt about owing anyone, especially her dad. "He didn't want to owe anyone, Dad, with law school and everything. Devon is trying to do the best he can, and as he said to me, your lawyer would cost a fortune. You know how Devon is. He pays his way, and the public defender's office is where he works. I don't know any more than that. Please tell me you're not going to say anything to Devon."

She watched as her dad pulled his hand over the back of his neck, and she knew that was his way of struggling with what he had to say. "You want me to stay out of it, Sara?"

Not what she expected, not from her dad. She fought with the word "yes" on the tip of her tongue and slid her gaze over to her brother, who appeared pensive, watchful, and brooding. "You mean if I told you to stay out of it, you would? Wow, Dad, that would really be something."

She wasn't sure if it was Gabriel who made the rude noise behind her dad, but he turned his head to the side, his expression amused.

"No, but I thought I would ask," Andy said. "Just remember something, both of you. You're my kids, so if something is bothering you, it's a problem for me."

Okay, so she had her answer. Would he stay out of it? Not likely.

Four

evon stared at the ring in the box, the red velvet and the cluster of diamonds. It screamed expensive, and at first glance, it appeared real.

"Wow, that's quite the ring!" said Kizzy Porter, a fellow intern with the public defender's office. "So I guess that answers my question—not single but taken. All the good ones are. I'm heartbroken, Devon. Guess there goes any chance I had with you, but then, they frown on workplace romances, especially when things go sour and the ex-couple is forced to work together day in and day out. Dislike soon turns to burning hatred, because the asshole side of people tends to come out, but you're forced to grin and bear it and paste a plastic smile on your face when all you want to do is scratch the other's eyes out. Yeah, guess it's for the best, although it could have been great."

He was still holding the ring box where he sat behind his cheap laminate desk, on a cloth padded chair with zero support, staring at Kizzy. Her desk was pushed against his and was stacked with files, papers, an endless caseload. Her skin was lighter than his, and the seams of her skirt and jacket pulled, likely from her squeezing her size-fourteen frame into a size twelve. It was just something that had stuck in his head when Sara pointed out to him the problems with women's dress sizes.

"Wow, you've got quite the imagination there, Kizzy," he said. "Hope that wasn't based on a current situation with someone here." He actually found himself looking around at the other lawyers and some clients.

"Nah," she said. "You're right, though. Coming up with a story, a good one, is something I've always been able to do. However, one of the cases I assisted on was in fact an attempted murder. Boy meets girl in the workplace, and they start a hot and dirty affair which ends very, very badly. She tried to stab him to death with a letter opener. She was aiming for his eye, but he turned his head, so she got him in the face. Nasty."

He didn't know what to say and wondered if the shock on his face was why she wore that amused grin. "Holy shit, seriously?"

She shrugged. "I would like to say I've seen and heard it all, but every day I'm more enlightened on all the idiotic things people will do in the name of love, money, family, or just surviving. It leaves me speechless. I actually have a journal where I keep a list of the most ridiculous and farfetched cases. I expected only one or two, but it's now over five pages, and I've been here only how long…?"

He blinked, wondering if she was deliberately trying to scare the shit out of him, before he pulled his gaze and took in the open ring box he was still holding. He was now torn on whether it was even right for Sara. He turned the ring box to Kizzy. "So, on to lighter and happier things, you don't think it's too much?"

She had pulled a file from the stack and opened it, flicking over it with a ballpoint pen, but she lifted her gaze. Her eyes, he noted, were blue, and every time she smiled, her dimples popped. "Well, since you're still holding it and haven't stuck it in a drawer after my words of wisdom, all I can think to ask now is, is she worth it?" She didn't pull her gaze away. She was intense, but then, she had to be if she wanted to be any good as a lawyer. There was something about her energy. He loved working alongside her.

"Completely, and then some." He snapped the box closed and set it in the middle of his desk, thinking of when he should ask Sara, considering he'd had the ring for nearly a month.

"Great! By the size of that rock, you'll be paying that off for the next ten plus years, so she better be, or it'll be just something else added to the divorce settlement when the chemistry dries up and you wake up one morning, see her face beside you on the other pillow, and ask yourself what the hell you were thinking."

"You're too young to be so jaded, Kizzy," Devon said. "Besides, if you knew Sara, you wouldn't say that. She's kind, sweet, awesome, the best—and the big rock is a fake diamond. The tiny ones you can barely see on the side are real, so not as expensive as you think. As you said, I don't want to be paying it off for the next ten years. I've got law school still, and rent, and a future with my girl. You think she'll be okay with a knockoff?"

Her smile softened. "From you, she'd be crazy not to. Smart, though, not spending your future on a piece of flashy jewelry. That's kind of a turn-on, Devon."

She was also a flirt. He'd never missed the interest, and it was kind of flattering, but at the same time, he wasn't interested. "Not sure about that," he said. "I thought girls liked the flash and glitter."

Kizzy was shaking her head. "Not this girl. Flash and glitter don't pay the electric bill or put food on the table or pay for things that really matter. Girls with any substance like a responsible and together guy who can stand on his own two feet and hold a job, one who doesn't take from her and is financially responsible instead of blowing everything as if there's no tomorrow. Just don't be that guy whose only desire is to meld himself into the sofa as if it's a second skin, getting up only to grab a second and third beer, watching TV until he goes to bed. You keep doing what you're doing. You're a catch and then some, Devon."

He suspected there was more to her comment, and she'd likely had a lot of personal issues with guys. "Ouch, sounds like you've had some bad luck?"

She was shaking her head as she looked at the file and jabbed the pen she was holding against it. "Oh, just my fate, I guess. I attract losers. Tell me, Devon, is the big old S for stupid still tattooed to my forehead?" She actually lowered her head as if to give him a good look before lifting her gaze again, and he couldn't help the laugh that only she could stir from him. She was smart, confident, with a sense of humor and a smart mouth that called everything as she saw it. He realized he'd never really taken the time to get to know her on a personal level.

"Nah, I think it's faded a bit," he said. "Just don't fall for all the flash and charm and nonsense that guys dish out. Remember, actions speak louder than words. If they can't back up all the bullshit with action, then keep walking."

She made a face again and pressed her lips together. "Great advice, Devon. Maybe I should invite you along when going on a date, and you can tell me if he's worthy or a deadbeat."

He was about to say sure, but then Burton Wade, the public defender who was handling his mom's case, was walking his way. Fit but five inches shorter than Devon, he had light hair parted at the side, and he wore tan slacks, a white shirt, and a tie in autumn colors.

"Devon, got a second? And bring the case files for Tiera Reed," was all he said as he stopped just behind Kizzy, who had turned in her chair.

"Yeah, sure," he said, and he slid back his chair and took in his boss's retreating back.

"Didn't he tell you yesterday to pack it up?" Kizzy kept her voice low, and he was grateful she didn't say anything else, considering everyone there knew that Tiera was his mother and the reason he'd decided on law school, putting everything he had into being a lawyer.

"He did. Said it was dead in the water, and he had more important cases to put his focus on. He said there was a point we had to cut our losses and move on, because my mom's case is just one of thousands, and he needed to focus on the ones he could actually win. I'm sure I'm leaving a few words out." He noted the shake of her head, her pensive gaze.

"Sounds like something I've heard around here too many times to count," she replied. Devon started around his desk, but Kizzy gestured to the ring box. "Oh, better pack up that knockoff.

Although you say it's not ridiculously expensive, it looks it, and I'd hate for it to go missing. I'm sure no one here would take it, but don't forget the number of people who come through here. The next client I have to meet with to go over his deposition has a rap sheet as long as my arm, mostly for pickpocketing."

He took in the red velvet box and reached over, then grabbed it and shoved it in his pocket. "Thanks," he said before he started across the office.

"Oh, and if you need some help on your mom's case, a second pair of eyes, just give me a shout. After all, I'm the one who finished top of my class. In other words, she may be your mom, but I can be objective, not to mention really good."

He took in Kizzy, the entire package—smart, brilliant, interesting. Yeah, if he wasn't already taken, he could definitely have seen himself pursuing something with her. "Thanks," he said again, and then he started across the office of five public defenders, four law students, and one overworked legal secretary.

Everyone was underpaid and had way too many cases. It was a wonder anyone could get a fair trial, and he couldn't help wondering what had happened to change Burton's mind about his mom. Burton was the most decisive lawyer in the office, a man who could easily have made a six-figure income out on his own but had chosen to stay overworked, underpaid, fighting to save those who couldn't afford the best of the best.

"So before I drag out all the boxes you asked me to pack…" Devon stopped talking and took in the two people he'd never expected to see in Burton's cramped, cluttered office: Andy Friessen, his girl's dad, and the lawyer who had once saved his ass. "Uh, I'm thinking I have my answer. Like, what is going on here?"

"So you know Jan Brown," Burton started, "and, of course, Andy Friessen, who has already pointed out to me that you're dating his daughter."

Living with his daughter, he wanted to correct as he angled his head to Andy, who wasn't smiling. He wanted to have a word with Sara, knowing she was likely the reason her dad was there.

"We all know each other, yes," Devon said. He nodded to Jan, an ordinary name for the extraordinary lawyer he'd met with two years earlier to start the process with his mom. Of course, he also couldn't help wondering if she'd shared with Andy any of the reasons why she wasn't on this case now.

"Great to see you, Devon," Jan said.

He turned to Andy. "This visit is about my mom's case," he said. He didn't even try to pose it as a question. It could have been just him and Andy in the room, without the other two lawyers. "Sara told you."

"Not in the way you think," he said. "I stopped by the site and overheard something, quizzed her. You know how I am with my family."

Oh, he did, all right. Andy was the kind of man who knew everything about them and what they were doing, anything that could hurt them. Devon still had a bit of road rash from the conversation he'd had with Andy when he'd asked Sara to move in, on his doorstep, in his face. No, he wouldn't mess up.

"Oh, I do, at that," Devon said. "So this is..." He started, then took in his boss, who was behind his desk, wearing the expression of a man who was being forced to do something he wasn't happy about.

"This is your mother's case being reopened," Burton said. He lifted his hand to Jan, who always had a look of confidence, with her short dark hair, navy suit, and eyes the color of taffy. "Jan is offering up her services, her time, and her resources. Merry Christmas, Devon. It seems it's your lucky day. It's not every day we have Jan Brown walking into the public defender's office to take over a case pro bono."

"Say what?" He turned his head so fast, taking in the smug expression on Andy's face and the confidence in Jan's.

"Just say thank you, Devon," Burton continued and strode around the desk to rest his hand on Devon's shoulder. Then, somehow, he had him turned and walking out of the office. "So go get those files, and while you're at it, take all of them into the conference room. You can set up and work with Jan in there. She's one of the heavyweights. This is a gift, Devon, and maybe Jan will be able to do something I couldn't."

Then Burton was walking away, over to one of the other public defenders who strode through the door with an armload of files piled atop a briefcase.

Sure, he should've been happy, but at the same time, he planned to have a heart to heart with Sara. The one thing that was a no-go for him was sharing anything that he talked about in confidence.

Nope, he loved her deeply, but at the same time, she needed boundaries where her dad was concerned. He'd make that clear. Otherwise, it would be something that could come between them.

CHAPTER

Five

Sara had pulled a scarf around her neck and slipped on the cream-colored wool hat from her purse. She felt the heater blowing behind her in the cold house as she went through the pages of notes, orders, quotes, and pricing for everything to see where she could cut some corners in the final budget.

"Sorry to dump all this on you," Gabriel said and leaned on the worktable across from her. He was covered in sawdust, packing it in for the day. Outside, behind the industrial lights in the house, the sunlight was waning as darkness settled in. She could hear the generator whirring and knew she'd have to turn it off before she left. The electrician was gone, and the posts would be as well, tomorrow, after the beam arrived. The two carpentry assistants who worked under Gabriel would be there to help him with the heavy lifting, and what followed would be a lot of swearing and some bumps and bruises. She'd make a point of coming later to avoid the drama.

She tapped her pen on the table and took in her

brother as she shrugged. "Part of the job. At least I get my open concept."

Well, that brought a smile, at least. At a sudden knock on the wooden beam, which echoed, he stood up and turned. "Devon, great to see you," he said. "And on that note, I'm out of here. Promised Elizabeth I'd be home before Shaunty's in bed tonight. Sara, see you tomorrow bright and early."

She just watched as he tapped his hand on Devon's shoulder, the exchange, the smile, and then Gabriel was gone.

Devon stepped in, wearing dark brown dress pants and a white dress shirt, his tie long gone, and a dark all-weather jacket. He took in the wood, the bare bones, and for a minute, she wondered if he was going to say anything. There was just something about him in that moment, but she knew he was angry. She'd expected him to still be at work, and she couldn't remember the last time he'd dropped by the job site to see her.

"I take it my dad..." she started, and he levelled everything on her. Yup, she'd nailed it. His dark eyes said he was pissed off, and he gave all of his energy to her, so she let the words hang.

"Sara, I shouldn't have to tell you there are some things you don't share. Everything we talk about is private. You don't run to your dad, your family, and share it. Private is private. You and me and what I share with you about my day, and the case with my mom, is between us. That wasn't up for discussion or for you to run to your dad and tell him. It had been parked and put away."

Oh, this was even worse. What had her dad done? "I'm sorry, and this isn't an excuse, but I didn't run to him, Devon. He overheard me venting this morning to Gabriel about how your mom's ex-boyfriend isn't willing to do the right thing…"

"So Gabriel knows too?" He cut her off, his voice lower, deeper, pissed off and angry. He took another step toward her and looked around, and she knew he was doing his best to pull it together.

"Oh, boy," she said. "Should I start by saying I'm sorry for caring and being pissed off for your mom, or for you because your mom is getting screwed over? I'm sorry, Devon. I would never deliberately share something personal between us, but I didn't think your mom's case being closed was something I had to hide. And again, I didn't run to my dad. I take it by how angry you are that you've talked to him? Evidently, he said something, did something."

Of course he had. She could tell by the way he angled his head, by the way he took her in and really looked.

"Yeah, he showed up with his lawyer, who's suddenly taking the case pro bono. You know how I feel about taking anything from your dad, him footing the bill for my mom…"

"Is he?" She couldn't let him finish. She knew Devon had a blind spot when he thought someone was trying to do him a kindness, as if he'd owe them everything. Devon didn't owe anyone anything.

He said nothing for a minute. "How else would she be there? You have any idea what her billable hours are? Good lawyers out here are two hundred to four hundred an hour, and she's four hundred and fifty, but she suddenly has time in her really busy schedule to devote all this time for free? Pro bono, really? I have a hard time with that one."

The way he said it, she knew he didn't believe it. She wondered if her dad was in fact paying her something. "What do you want me to say, Devon, that I'm sorry for caring? I'm not, if it means your mom will get a fair shake. No one deserves to be paying for something she didn't do. She's been in prison a lot of years, Devon. Don't you think you should take the help, be happy for it? Because I am."

He ran his hand over his face and groaned. She could see his frustration and hear how he was fighting, needing to be angry over something he shouldn't be. But pride was pride with a man like Devon. She knew that.

"Sara, I need to know that when I share something with you, you're not going to run to your dad, your brother, your family. I'll have your word on that. Put aside my mother and all of this, because this comes down to a matter of trust, and you know how important that is to me."

She took in the papers and her laptop, feeling the sting of the reprimand. "You know you have it. I'm sorry, Devon. Honestly, I didn't think the closed case was in the no-talk zone."

There it was, the twitch of his lips, and he took another step until he was right in front of her and she had to look up at him. She pressed her hand to his chest, feeling gritty and seeing how tired he looked.

"So can I ask you where it stands now with the reopened case," she said, "or am I going to find myself sitting in the penalty box now, with you not sharing what you can?"

This time he laughed. "Penalty box, really? Wow,

quite the way with words there, Sara. No, you're not excluded, but don't tell your dad. I'm having a hard enough time understanding how his lawyer suddenly wants to be involved in a case she made clear was a loser from the start."

She wasn't sure what to make of what Devon had said, and she wondered if the confusion showed on her face.

"Your dad put me in touch with her two years back," Devon explained. "We met, we talked, and she looked into it, but it was never going to work with her."

So that was why he'd worked it out with the public defender, pushing and putting in all those hours. She had known there was more, but she'd never questioned the change. Maybe she should have. "Why would you say that? Your mom didn't do it."

Devon stepped back and strode in a circle, running his hand over the back of his neck. It was a motion she was familiar with, especially when the tension ratcheted up a notch or two.

"Devon, answer me. This isn't one of those things we can't talk about."

He was shaking his head as he took her in. "It was just something she said."

She said nothing more as she waited, her arms crossed, her fingers digging into her skin through her down coat. "Come on, Devon. Normally, I can wait, but this is…"

"She asked me if my mom wasn't better off being left there in jail, considering that if she got out, there was a high probability she'd be right back into the drugs, the crime, hooking up with yet another loser. What would she have going for her, just me and Anton? And maybe this time she'd drag us into the gutter with her, as if we'd be talked into doing something stupid. Your dad's lawyer seemed convinced it could land on me, hurt me, and the next time it would be me, Anton, or both of us locked up with my mom."

She just stared in horror, and for a second, she couldn't speak.

He shrugged again. "Sometimes, Sara, people don't believe someone can really change. Yeah, my mom was a shitty mom, and she'd done other stuff, but saying she deserved what she got is pretty fucking cold."

"And you told my dad?" Sara said. She thought her voice squeaked, and for a second she believed he had to have misunderstood.

He shook his head. "Nope, it was his lawyer who said it. Your dad was trying to help. He's not responsible for what she believes."

"You've got to tell him," she said, but this time Devon was adamant. She knew his expression. He had set his mind to believing it and couldn't be talked into seeing another way.

"Nope," he said.

"Well, I can see your predicament and why you'd think my dad is paying her, so what are you going to do?"

He pulled in a breath and said nothing for a second. It was in that lingering silence with Devon that she always struggled. What was he thinking, doing, holding on to? Then he reached into his jacket and pulled out a red velvet box. He flicked it open, and she stared at the ring he was now holding out to her. All she could do was stare like a fool, feeling her heart drop to her knees.

"I'm going to ask my girl to spend the rest of her life with me."

She knew her mouth was gaping open, feeling her hands on her cheeks, in shock, stunned, and she lifted her gaze to Devon, wanting all of this but not expecting it, considering they'd just been talking about his mother.

"Well, you're going to make me do this the hard way on this sawdusty floor," he said, and then he pulled his pant leg up with one hand and went down on his knee, and she stared at the ring, at him. "Sara Friessen, you're the love of my life, and I want to spend the rest of my life with you. Please say yes and marry me."

Then the generator clunked, and the lights went out, and they were suddenly in a cold room in the dark.

"The gas can is empty," Sara said as she returned from checking the generator, holding a large plastic red jerry can.

Devon shone his cell phone out the door. It was fully dark outside now aside from the streetlights. There was something about a house during construction: Everything echoed, including the sound of the gas can Sara dropped at his feet. "Well, just lock it up," he said. "Let's go. You're done here, right?"

He watched her walk over to the workbench, where she lifted a big flashlight from beside the chop saw and piles of tools. When she flicked it on, it lit up the room.

He'd been kneeling like a fool before all the lights went out, but he'd since tucked the ring back in his jacket pocket, the moment lost.

Sara walked over to another workbench, where her papers and laptop were sitting, and he took a second to really see the bare bones of the house, surveying what she and Gabriel had done.

"I can do the rest at home," she said. "I have to go

through everything and rework all the numbers to cut close to fifteen grand from all the finishes. Any idea how hard that is? I've already planned out the design and ordered things, including appliances. I've picked the colors, a theme that flows from one room to the next, and everything ties in nicely. I'm basically starting over, having to scrap what I envisioned and do something different. That's weeks of work down the drain. Then I have to rework the numbers and suddenly become cheap, which, in designing, is really difficult."

He had no idea what she'd put into this, but he could see how much she loved what she did and wondered what kind of money she was used to working with. He cleared his throat. "In a manner of speaking, I know exactly what you mean."

She shoved the last of the papers into her bag and lifted it over her shoulder, shining the flashlight over to the door. It hit him and blinded him for a second, and he lifted his hand to cover his eyes as he shut them. "Whoa, there! Shine that light somewhere else, not in my face."

"Sorry," she said. "Can you grab the gas can for me while I lock up? Toss it in the back of the pickup, and I'll get some gas in the morning on the way here."

"Sure, need me to take anything else?" He reached for the can, shining his cellphone flashlight, and stepped out onto the cement block front stoop.

"Nope, I've got everything. I just sent Gabriel a text to thank him for making sure the generator was full before leaving."

He glanced over his shoulder, seeing her in the shadows and not missing the sarcasm in her voice. Then she was walking his way. The neighborhood was quiet, middle class, the kind of place he'd never felt at home in. He pictured the white-collar crowd, and one glance at the lights shining from the homes told him what kind of community this was and gave him a clearer idea of what Sara did. This was the kind of place that was made for her, where she would fit in nicely. But him…he just couldn't picture himself here. It just didn't fit.

He opened the back door of her pickup and rested the can on the floor, then closed the door just as Sara appeared, shining the beam of the flashlight wide. He opened the driver door for her, scanning over the pickup her dad had given her, which had the kinds of bells and whistles he'd never be able to afford, not on an intern's salary, with the mountain of debt he had to pay off.

"Thank you," she said, resting her hand on the door. "So, listen. We were interrupted."

He touched her chin, leaned in, and pressed a kiss to her lips before pulling back, for the first time worried about who may have seen and about the appropriateness of kissing her. It was silly and made no sense, but he wasn't about to explain it to Sara. He knew there were so many times she just didn't understand how different it was for her, for him.

"Let's get out of here," he said. "It's cold. We'll talk at home." Then he'd be able to get his nerve up again, pop the question, give her the ring, and make dinner with his girl, after which he could hit the books and then stumble to bed for a few hours of sleep. Or maybe it could wait—should wait. He needed to think this proposal thing through again.

He followed her home to the apartment he shared with Anton, and it wasn't lost on him how different their busy, chaotic neighborhood felt. Things happened here that wouldn't in the kind of neighborhood where Sara's renovation project was situated. He locked up his Mazda, where the oil light was perpetually on. The miles had clicked past four hundred thousand, and he wondered how much longer it would be before he'd have to drive it to the junkyard and scrape together money he didn't have for something in better shape, better condition, something that still ran.

He took in the darkened parking lot, the cars, the concrete, the seclusion on the way to the back door they always went through, where the lightbulb was still burnt out. There was no one around to hear if something went wrong.

"What are you looking at?" Sara said as she came around the pickup to find him holding his briefcase in one hand and his keys in the other.

"See the super still hasn't fixed the light," he said. He watched as Sara started walking to the door, her bag looped over her shoulder and her cellphone flashlight on.

"I don't think that light has ever worked, not as long as I've lived here," Sara said. "Boy, you really have been distracted. Not a biggie. Just have your cellphone light on while you walk and your keys ready."

He spotted the lock and shoved his key in as she shone the light, then held the door for her. Sara walked in under his arm, shorter, gorgeous. He wanted to make sure no harm came near her as he took in the concrete hallway, which was dimly lit. What was it about following her now that had him really looking at every-thing? He'd never considered any of this to be a problem for himself.

"Elevator is out," Sara said, and he took in the

handwritten paper taped to the elevator door, which read, *Out of order: Take the stairs!*

He took in the lobby, old, worn. The front glass door should have been locked, but it was propped open by a piece of wood. He kicked the block out and pulled it closed so the lock clicked.

"How often is the door open? Anyone could walk in," he said, then took in the way Sara was watching him. She shrugged, and he ran his hand over his short cropped hair, feeling the urgency of everything that was outside his control. Something about driving in there tonight in the dark with Sara had made him realize this wasn't the ideal place for a woman like her to live.

"I don't know, a few times," she said. "Mostly someone bringing stuff in and not wanting to dig their keys out for all the loads they're carrying, you know, groceries and things. Doesn't matter. At least we're not hauling groceries up five flights." She tapped his chest with the flat of her hand and rubbed, flicking those mischievous green eyes up to him as if all of this was no big deal. "Not sure I'd want to be carrying groceries tonight, so I'm glad I went shopping yesterday."

He followed her as she started ahead of him up the concrete stairwell. It was isolated, the perfect spot for someone to be attacked, robbed. "You happy living here?"

She tossed him a distracted glance. "That's an odd thing to ask me. What's prompted this question? Of course, I love being with you."

"I didn't mean with me. I meant living in this place." He followed behind her, and she glanced back at him from the next landing.

"Your point? I'm afraid I don't get it."

"Oh, I guess I started thinking after seeing the house you and your brother are working on. It's safe there in suburbia," he said. White suburbia, he suspected, but he didn't add that part. "And then there's this old place where Anton and I live. I was never worried before about coming and going. It was affordable and doable for me and Anton, but now, seeing the broken-down elevator, the back light out, this stairwell, the perfect spot for someone to hide…"

It was a good thing he was in such good shape, as he could keep up with Sara as she opened the fifth-floor door and glanced back to him. He saw the hesitation and something else in her expression.

"You're suddenly worried something could happen to me?" she said. "I can look after myself, Devon. It's not as if I've just moved in. We talked about this before when you asked me to move in, remember? So did my dad. You both worried about me being attacked or hurt or walking into some sort of danger, but I reminded you that I'm not usually coming home in the middle of the night, and the front door is usually locked, and it's not as if this building is the scene of endless drug deals, stabbings, robberies, murders, or any other miscellaneous crimes. I know the neighbors. They're good people."

As he followed Sara down the hallway, he took in the doors of neighbors he didn't know, because he'd always kept his head down so as not to attract attention. Yeah, he definitely wasn't comfortable. She shoved her key into the deadbolt and unlocked it, and he took a second to really see the hall, the dirty, dingy carpet that looked like puke, and lighting that could have been better. He could hear TVs and noise from behind a few of the doors. Who were these people Sara was talking to?

"Just the same, maybe we should consider moving," he said as he closed the door behind them. The TV was on, video games blasting. Anton was playing some shooter. Of course he was home. He was always there, considering his nine to five at the pawn shop around the corner was more like a ten to three. Just another thing he hadn't put a ton of thought into.

Sara shrugged out of her coat and tossed it on a hook at the door, then pulled off her wool hat and scarf. The entry was cramped and cluttered. Her expression was amused, surprised. "Devon, I told you before it doesn't matter where we live, but if you want to move…" She let it hang, and he didn't miss the hope that lingered in her voice. She walked through the kitchen, taking in the sink filled with dirty dishes and what looked like fish sticks on a cookie sheet on the stove, and he was positive she uttered a certain four-letter word. "Anton, you planning on cleaning up or leaving it for me to do?"

He felt the velvet box inside his jacket and rested his briefcase on the table, which was covered in mail, a newspaper, and a dirty plate.

"Yeah, yeah, I'll get to it," Anton said. "Don't get your panties in a knot."

Devon lifted his head, seeing his brother glued to the TV, and Sara tensed, ready to say something. What was it about Sara and Anton? He swore they'd never get along.

"Hey, Anton," was all he had to say as he jabbed his thumb to the kitchen behind him. His brother looked his way and then rolled his eyes before pausing the game and tossing the controller on the sofa.

He wondered then, seeing the way his brother

looked at Sara, the dislike he didn't try to hide. When had it turned so bad? With their personalities, the two of them were like a match and gasoline, not safe for anyone to be around. The fine line he had to walk with both of them was just something else he needed to handle—and he still needed to talk to his brother about his mom's case, which he did on an almost daily basis.

"Nag, nag, nag," Anton muttered. "Never happened before she moved in here—and might I remind you," he said, turning to Sara, "my name's on the lease, which means you're the guest here."

Sara stiffened.

"Show some respect, Anton," Devon said. "Sara is not a guest here. She lives here with me. We've talked about this, and I told you how I feel. Before Sara moved in, I told you I could move out and get my own place with her, but do you remember what you said?"

His brother banged around in the sink, lifting dirty dishes out as if he was going to wash them. "I know, but I thought you'd come to your senses," Anton said. "The two of you don't fit. She's not from our world, Devon, but here she is, living here anyway. And then look at you, acting like you're trying to find a way to fit into hers. We're brothers, man. Where's your loyalty to me, to Mom?"

Devon didn't have to look back at Sara to know how angry she was. Anton just didn't seem to get how he loved her. "You know what, Anton? That's not cool. Yeah, we're brothers, but this isn't a contest of who I like more. She's my girl. I'm not picking anyone over the other. What's wrong with you? And another thing, Sara's not here to clean up after either of us, and I'm tired of the bickering between the two of you." He tossed a glance back to Sara and didn't miss the way she stiffened. "I just want some damn peace around here. I don't want to have to come home and soothe either of your feelings after you ruffle each other's feathers. I don't think there's been a night I walked in without seeing you two at each other's throats, so maybe it's time Sara and I moved out."

He wasn't sure who was more shocked, his brother or Sara.

"And another thing…" he started, reaching into his jacket pocket and pulling out the ring box. He held it out and didn't have to look Anton's way to sense his shock. Hell, he couldn't believe what he was doing. "I could wait, but I need to be clear, Anton. Sara's not going away."

He flicked open the box again and this time faced Sara, who now had an odd expression. He wasn't sure if she was ready to slug him or kiss him. He felt as if he were walking through a minefield, without a clue where the bombs were planted.

"Come on, Sara. You never answered me," he said. He knew his brother was standing right behind him from the way Sara's wide eyes took in the box and then glanced past him.

"Are you seriously popping the question?" Anton said, and he sounded like such an asshole, reaching for the ring box.

Devon slapped his brother's hand. "No, no, hands off! This isn't your business, Anton."

"Hey…" Anton said.

Devon put all the irritation he was feeling into the gaze he sent his brother's way as he said, "Don't you have dishes to do?" Then he took in Sara, who was just standing there, saying nothing. She wasn't smiling, so he reached for her hand and pulled her with him to their bedroom.

"Devon, what are you doing?" she finally said, tugging at her hand.

He pulled her into the cramped room and closed the door. Their bedroom had one dresser, and his and mostly her clothes were crammed into a closet where the doors wouldn't close. Most of her things were still stacked in a box in the corner. Yeah, they definitely needed more space, their own space.

"I asked you to marry me earlier tonight," he said, "and yeah, the lights went out, but now here we are, and you haven't said a word."

Her arms were crossed, and he was trying to figure out where her head was from the way she glared at him. Pissed off? Yes. A woman ready to say yes? No.

"You think I'm the one causing all this shit and problems with your brother?" she said.

Oh, here we go. Sara and Anton hating each other was the last thing he wanted to deal with now. It was beginning to feel like a tug of war, and he was expected to choose a side. "I never said that, Sara. You're putting words in my mouth. But he's my brother. Are you expecting me to choose between the two of you?"

The minute he said that, she took a step back. He was stilling gripping that ring box, so he finally tossed it on the bed and ran his hands over his face, frustrated. He groaned, pulled his hands away, and took in her expression, and hurt was all he saw.

"It's not that simple, Devon. You think I don't know that he hates me?"

"He doesn't hate you. That's overkill. You two are too much alike, is the problem."

She made a face of disgust. "We are not alike, Devon."

He actually laughed. "Oh, you are. Neither of you wants to bend and get along. You both want what you want. He's always looked after me, so I'm not going to kick him to the curb…"

"But you're ready to kick me?" She cut him off, and he shook his head, lifting his hands and squeezing his fists, seeing this going around and around, never resolving anything.

"No, I'm not kicking either of you. I just want you to get along, please. That's all I've ever asked, Sara."

"It's not all on me, Devon. You heard him out there, the way he spoke to me, the way he came at me with that disrespect…"

"And how do you talk to him, Sara? I'll tell you how: the same way. He does something you don't like, and you just can't ignore it. Last night, I walked in to see you'd ripped the TV cord from the wall, and you were standing there looking like a crazy person. And before you go off on me about how it wasn't just you, I know it takes two. But you need to meet him halfway."

She just stared at him. He didn't want to have to keep his girl and his brother separate. And then there was his mom. How was she going to fit in with all this?

"I'm not going to let your brother walk all over me and disrespect me," she said.

No, he knew she wouldn't. He shook his head. "He won't. I'll talk to him. But ease up, please."

She looked around, and the hard set of her jaw reminded him so much of her dad. Then her green eyes fell on him before she glanced at the ring on the bed, and she leaned down and reached for the box. He wasn't sure what she was about to do, close it up and hand it back to him? The way his night was going, he feared she'd say no or nothing at all.

But she didn't. Instead, she lifted the ring out of the box and held it out to him.

"You want to ask me again, and maybe put it on my finger this time?" she said.

He took the ring from Sara and took in the big fake rock, the gold band, and the tiny specks of diamonds. He hesitated again. "You want to get married?"

She gave him an odd look.

"Come on, Sara. Say you'll marry me." He held her hand and took in the way her gaze lingered.

"Of course I'll marry you," she said.

He slid the ring on her finger and then pulled her close, wrapping his arms around her and over her ass. Her arms looped around his neck, over his shoulders, and he lifted her, kissing her deeply, tasting her, wanting nothing more than to lay her down on the bed, strip her, and show her how much he wanted her, but she stopped and broke the kiss, pulling in one breath and then another, still smiling.

"Oh, and don't forget you'll need to ask my dad," she said.

He let his arms loosen and nearly dropped her. "Say what?"

She squealed as she slid down and hit the floor, then said, "Yeah, you know, he's kind of expecting you to come to him and ask him if you can marry me."

Maybe it was the shock on his face that had her

laughing softly, teasingly, and for a second he thought she was kidding. "Seriously?"

She nodded and lifted her hand, taking in the sparkling ring. "Afraid so. Even though we're living together, this is just one of those things my dad expects you to talk to him about. You still want to marry me?" She flicked those amazing green eyes up to him again, and he realized she was serious. Like, how old school was this?

He exhaled and looked around. "Fine, so I talk to your dad and ask what? Like, permission to marry you like you're a piece of property or something?" He realized by the look on her face that she'd taken it the wrong way, or maybe the right way.

"No, that's got nothing to do with it, Devon. It's about respect and the fact that I'm his daughter and he's always looked after all of us—my mom, me, Chels, my brothers. He's there for us, and he just wants to be sure that you're good enough for me," she said and shrugged, and he realized how complex this all was. He thought he'd figured her family out, how he fit with them, but there was always something new that he'd never expected.

"So this is really about the formality of me standing in front of your dad…"

"Man to man," she added, as if he needed help figuring it out.

He groaned, knowing her dad wouldn't make anything easy. "He wouldn't say no, would he?"

Sara took a step and pressed her hands over his chest, really looking at him, confident, smart, teasing, while he worried about what she might say. "No, of course not, but you should know by now that with my dad, there's no easy road. He may make you sweat a bit."

Great, just what he wanted. Andy would likely make him sit there and wait for an answer, sweating and wondering, before proceeding to tell him all the ways he expected him to make sure his daughter was happy. "Of course he will," he said.

Sara just shrugged. "It's who he is. But then we can talk about the wedding and make plans…oh, and just so you know, my parents expect a wedding, a real one, where Dad can give me away and Mom can fuss over me."

He just stared at Sara, because even though he wanted to marry her and live together, what he hadn't considered was the dollar signs he was now seeing. First there was the matter of paying full rent on a new place, and now what would a wedding end up costing him?

He knew he was late as he hurried down the concrete steps and pulled open the glass door to the public defender's office, but he'd slept through his alarm after tossing and turning all night. He'd just stared at Sara, remembering what Kizzy had said about money and being realistic.

Now here he was, far from rested, feeling unprepared and picturing all the files he hadn't gotten to, as he'd allowed Anton and his ruffled feathers to distract him while he cranked up the sound on the TV, with the guns and the shooting, not stopping until two a.m.

His hair was still damp, but at least he'd taken the time for a shower before racing out the door in a pair of black jeans and a gray dress shirt, all the clean clothes he had left, while Sara stumbled from bed and made coffee. Anton had still been asleep.

He spotted Jan in the conference room, and Burton was with her. He knew he had only seconds before they spotted him, so he raced past it to the back of the office, to the corner where his desk was. Kizzy had her head down but jerked up when she spotted him.

"You're late," she said. "Burton's been looking for you, and he didn't sound happy that you weren't here yet. If you'd given me a heads-up, I could have made an excuse for you."

He shrugged out of his coat and tossed it over his chair as he dumped his briefcase on his desk, and he didn't miss her taking in what he was wearing. "Not up to you to lie for me," he said. "Don't worry about it, Kizzy."

She nodded, still staring at him, her lips firmed. "I didn't know it was casual dress-down Tuesday."

He pulled out the files he'd taken home yet hadn't looked at, the papers spilling over his desk. "Yeah, well, last night was just one of those nights beyond my control. This is all I have clean. Laundry is piling up, and I haven't had a chance to do a load…"

"Devon!"

He looked up to see Burton barreling his way, digging into each step, his tie swinging, his white shirt crisp and ironed. The way he gestured, Devon could tell he was on a short fuse today, so he wondered what else was up.

"If you're done gossiping, you think you can give us your time? Or do you expect two senior lawyers to stand around all day and wait for you to show up and actually do the work you're supposed to be here doing?"

He'd never been on the receiving end of a full-force tongue lashing from Burton. "Sorry, of course, I'll be right there," he said, but Burton had turned and was already on his way back to the conference room.

Kizzy looked up at him—supportive, he thought, and curious. "You pop the question? She said no?"

He shook his head and grabbed his legal notepad and pen. He didn't have a second to waste. "No, she said yes." He tried to smile. "It's just all this. I'd better not keep the boss waiting, or I'll find my ass kicked out of here. How long have they been in there?"

She turned to the conference room. "A few hours, at least. Jan Brown was here before me, and Burton came in right after. You know I'm usually here before everyone. Apparently, she wanted an early start. You'd better run."

He didn't linger, but as he took a step, she reached over and touched his arm.

"Hey, listen," she said. "Why don't we have drinks tonight, and you can tell me all about your proposal, how it went?"

He took in her smile. At the same time, he could see Jan and Burton talking. He sensed they were waiting for him, which wasn't a good thing. "Yeah, sure. Listen, I'll catch up to you later," he said, distracted.

He hurried to the conference room, seeing the boxes he'd once packed up on the table, files open. No one was smiling. "Sorry to be late. It was a… Sorry. It won't happen again." He stopped talking, because the last thing they or anyone wanted was to listen to a pile of excuses from a law student. Jan was willingly taking him under her wing as a favor to Andy, taking on a case that, until the previous day, had been dead in the water.

"Devon, let's be clear," Burton said. "Everyone is here putting time in for you, and you're just a second-year law student. Make sure you're not late again."

He felt the bite and took in his boss, the way he

glanced to his watch before giving all his attention to Jan, who was quiet and watchful.

"I need to be in court," Burton said, then let his gaze land on Devon and said nothing more before he nodded and left the room.

Devon took in Jan, who was dressed in a brown twill pantsuit and a ruffled white blouse, her sleeves rolled up. Only her left ring finger was missing a ring.

"So, Devon, I've had a chance to go through all the files and get myself up to speed again. It's been a long time since I saw the details, but it didn't take long to come back to me. Let's just say it's as I remembered, quite the uphill battle. I reviewed all your notes and your mother's confession, and I agree with you and Burton that going after the boyfriend and getting him to come clean is the easiest course of action. Or is there something else I should be looking at? Tell me."

He took a seat in one of the six mismatched chairs around the conference table, which was actually two cheap plywood tables shoved together, and he took in the whiteboard, which she'd filled with notes, a timeline, cops' names, and gun models. Under Darnell's name was a list of what he thought were questions. She really had been there a while.

"So why did you suddenly want to help with this case—and pro bono, too?" he said.

She stilled, looking down at him from where she stood at the end of the table. Her taffy-colored eyes gave him the impression that everyone underestimated how sharp she was. "You care to elaborate?" she replied.

He said nothing for a second, taking in her direct manner. It was soft, the way she spoke, but he felt the punch with her every word. "Okay, let's put it all out on the table. I remember what you said. You seemed to think my mother was better off left in jail, because there's a high probability she'd be right back into the drugs, the crime, hooking up with yet another loser. Pretty sure those were your exact words. Oh, yeah, and you seemed to think she'd drag me and Anton down with her, as if we don't know right from wrong, and we too would find ourselves behind bars. She doesn't need someone working on her behalf who doesn't believe in her."

She didn't say a word. In fact, she stood there, one hand across her waist and the other clicking a pen. Her dark hair was short, neat, not a strand out of place. Her earrings were simple elegant pearls, and she lifted a brow. Her makeup was light. She reached for a mug he hadn't noticed on the conference room table and lifted it to her lips, then swallowed. He thought she was doing her best not to laugh, which only made him angry.

"So why are you really here?" he continued. "You say it's pro bono, but I'm thinking it's more that Andy Friessen is footing the bill for all your time. I know him. I know how he likes to stick his nose in my business, in everyone's."

She flicked her gaze over to him and still hadn't answered, and he didn't have a clue what she was thinking. Then she pulled in a breath around a smile he suspected she used in the courtroom.

"Devon, first, if I agree to do pro-bono work, that's exactly what it is. No one buys me, and there's no ruse where Andy is paying for me unbeknownst to you. I assure you I'm here willingly—yes, at Andy's urging, because, as he pointed out, I need a certain number of pro-bono hours a month. This is it for me. He asked, and I said yes. If I recall, I was the one who originally reopened this case. While we're putting all our cards out on the table and calling a spade a spade, might I also ask, is that why you pulled the case from me and brought it over here to Burton?"

"Sounds like you don't think Burton's any good," he snapped.

She smiled, wolf-like. "No, Burton is very good, but, being a public defender, he's limited in what he can do in terms of time, resources, even with you helping and doing all the work in the background. Yes, I see all the notes, the briefs, the research—all done by you. Let me remind you that up until yesterday, when I walked in here with Andy, Burton had closed this case and packed these files away. So what's the real issue, Devon?" She had such control and confidence in her voice.

"You think an innocent woman belongs in jail. That's what you said to me," he snapped.

She opened her mouth to say something, then let out a breath that sounded like a sigh. "No, Devon, I don't, and I'm not sure how you got that from me. I don't believe anyone belongs in jail for something they didn't do. Unfortunately, the prisons are filled with people who find themselves doing time for crimes they didn't commit, but your mother's case is complicated by the fact that she chose to take the fall for a man who tossed her to the curb. She fell for the lies and willingly walked away from you and your brother. She's got a lot riding against her."

He just gestured toward her, feeling the anger pulse through him. She was saying exactly the same thing as before.

"I can tell you're not hearing me," Jan said, "so

before you up and fire me again, I want you to really listen to me this time. What you're not understanding, and what I meant to say, is that she's been through a terrible trauma. Being locked up does things to people that you and I can't understand. The years she's been living behind bars, she's had her freedom taken from her, her rights, her dignity. Everything that makes you and me civilized has been yanked from her, and she's had to figure out how to survive in there. It's different in prison, how you live, how you see the world. She likely won't have the coping skills to get by out here." She motioned between them, and he felt a sick feeling tighten in his stomach.

"Hey, on the bright side," she continued, "let's look at the reality of the situation. We'll lean on the boyfriend, get him to come clean and give us the details of the guns, where he got them, and we'll take it to a judge. Maybe there'll be a new trial, and then she'll be out. At the same time, what I'm trying to say to you—and, evidently, you didn't hear me before—is that getting out won't be enough. In the outside world, in this life that you and I handle, she'll be a social pariah, essentially unemployable. From that, she'll be headed in a downward spiral. She'll be drawn right to the same things that landed her behind bars, the drugs, the no-good boyfriends, because they'll see how broken she is. Are you understanding what I'm saying? This isn't a new story. In fact, it's an old one, carved out by ex-con after ex-con. The deck is stacked against her."

He gestured to her. "Then why are you here? Because from what you're saying, it sounds as if you believe it's a waste of your time, everyone's time, to get her out. You're making it sound as if everyone who gets out of jail doesn't make it, and that isn't true. There are those who turn everything around."

This time, an odd smile touched her lips, and the soft laugh under her breath was unnerving. "I didn't say everyone, so don't misunderstand me or put words in my mouth. Yes, there are a few who actually go on to build really successful lives, get married, have kids, start a career, get fame and fortune. But that isn't something that happens often, and the difference is that many of them have done the crime and admitted to it. They come clean and turn their lives around because they say there's no way they'll ever go back to that. Your mom isn't about to walk out of there without a scratch on her. She'll need help, therapy, counselling, a lot of it, and all of that is going to cost money. Are you prepared to foot that bill? You need to understand all of this. Am I making sense? Do you get it now? No one, especially in a broken system, is going to say, 'Okay, we screwed you up. Here, we're going to help fix you now.'"

The way she said it, he could see she was a tough-as-nails lawyer that only Andy Friessen would retain. He understood how he'd misread her back then. Or had he?

"Maybe it won't be as hard as you think," he said. "She won't be alone."

She would have Anton, and him, and then there was Sara—but he didn't add that part, because he wasn't sure about having his mom around her.

"Well, let's get to work and get your mother out of jail," Jan said. She leaned on the boardroom table and seemed to be considering something. "But one more thing, Devon. I want your word that if you have a problem with something I do or say, you come to me and you ask me. Don't throw away another two years when your mom could be out already."

He got the bite. This was all on him. It was his fault his mom was still in jail.

"So we're good?" she said.

He pulled in a breath, stuck on her words. "We're good," he finally said, but were they? If Jan was right, he realized that while his mom may have lied to get herself in jail, his arrogance was what had kept her there.

"So where is he?" was all her dad said as he strode into the kitchen. He didn't walk in like a normal person. Every time he moved, it was with purpose, and she didn't miss the demand in his voice. His arms were gritty, and he turned on the kitchen tap to wash up. The black sleeves of his shirt were pushed up, and he wore a navy down vest overtop and faded blue jeans. Even his perpetual five o'clock shadow added to the pissed-off expression he'd worn since glimpsing the ring on her finger as she drove in past where he'd been shoveling manure in the round ring out front.

"Working, likely," she replied. "He said he'd be here, but…"

Devon was more often late than not. She realized the life of a law student didn't run from nine to five, which was why she'd sent him a reminder text before leaving the job site. When she hadn't heard from him after parking at the ranch, she'd sent another.

She heard the ding of her phone then and pulled it from her back pocket, seeing the text: *Sorry, on my way.*

She held the butcher knife and continued to chop the celery her mom had added to the pile of vegetables she was working through.

Hearing a vehicle, she glanced out the kitchen window to see that Gabriel, Elizabeth, and Shaunty were there.

"You should be happy he's so dedicated, Dad," Sara said. "At least he's not a drifter without ambition. Devon gives everything to his studies, to school, to working, to becoming a lawyer."

She could see, though, that in his dedication he could end up sacrificing her. She lifted her gaze and took in her mom, her light hair hiked up in a high ponytail, wearing a light green sweater. She took her in, her glance unamused. Something was on her mind.

Her dad shook off the water on his hands and reached for a towel, then turned and leaned against the sink, unsmiling.

"Sara, we like Devon a lot," Laura said. "We always have, but your dad is right. He should be here." She turned to her husband. "Andy, you need to ease up. Even you said to me how much you admire Devon and how he's taken on his mom's case and hasn't given up."

Had her dad really said that? She looked over to her parents, seeing the exchange just as the door opened and voices flooded in.

"Hey, Grandma, Grandpa!" cried Brandon, her five-year-old nephew. She hadn't seen him come over, but he raced into the house with Shaunty. Elizabeth followed, wearing a striped shirt and blue jeans. She could hear what she thought was Jeremy and Gabriel talking.

"So what's going on?" Elizabeth asked, having guessed from Andy and Laura's expressions and the heaviness that lingered. Her long dark hair was hanging loose, and her eyes went from Sara to them, taking them all in, waiting for someone to say something.

"Oh, Devon and I are getting married," Sara said, "and Dad is a little pissed because he didn't come and talk to him first." She lifted her hand just as her brothers strode in, dressed ranch casual, their expressions interested. Everyone took a second to look at her ring. Tiffy, whom she hadn't heard come in, squealed and took in her hand before hugging her. The only one missing was her younger brother, Zac.

"Wow, gorgeous!" Tiffy said. "Look at the size of that rock. Mine's tiny in comparison." Tiffy lifted her hand, showing the decent-sized diamond. Her ring was the first one Andy had given Laura, and Laura had passed it along to Jeremy. Elizabeth also lifted her hand, showing off her gold band with a few tiny diamonds. Sara didn't have to look over to her brothers to know they weren't impressed.

"A rock isn't everything, but I think your mom has us all beat," Elizabeth said.

They all turned to Laura, who was wearing a simple diamond band. The huge rock her dad had bought for her several anniversaries earlier was sitting in her jewelry box, worn only when she wasn't in the kitchen, cleaning, or helping with any of the barnyard chores. It was the kind of ring that cost a small fortune.

"It's not real," Jeremy said from among everyone who stood around the island in the kitchen. Even Shaunty had squeezed in to have a look at Sara's finger.

"That's ridiculous," Sara said. "Of course it's real. Look at it."

Everyone now seemed to be studying it closer except for her mom and dad.

"It better not be," Andy said. "A rock that size would cost an easy forty, fifty grand, and I know the debt load Devon is carrying already with school."

Everyone looked over to Andy, and Sara noted the way her mom stared up at him. She had a way of saying everything with just a look.

"He's got a good head on his shoulders," Andy said. "It's a good thing he's not tossing out forty grand on a ring, because that would be just plain stupid, considering he has less than nothing. If he wants a future with you, he needs to be practical and save so he can put something away for you two and get you out of that dive of an apartment."

No one said anything. She stared at her dad, who was clearly in a mood. She'd never before heard him talk that way, and she couldn't help feeling disappointment at the doubt Jeremy had created.

"Why would you say it's fake? It's not fake." She held it up and was about to pull it off her finger to take a look at it when she heard a car in the drive. Her dad turned to glance out the window along with her mom.

"Devon's here," he said.

"Be nice," Laura replied before anyone could say anything, pressing her hand to Andy's chest and holding him there a second. It was a sight to see, her petite mom holding her tall, strong dad in place.

"I'm always nice," Andy said, which had Jeremy and Gabriel laughing.

Sara rolled her eyes. Brandon and Shaunty were both standing beside her, still appearing far too interested in her ring, so Laura scooted them both out of the kitchen. She heard Devon on the steps and heard the knock on the screen door before it squeaked open, and Devon and her mom were talking.

He was still laughing as he appeared in the kitchen. "Hey, y'all. Sorry I'm late," he said.

She took in his blue jeans and dark shirt as he slid off his coat, his expression harried. He nodded to Jeremy and Gabriel, and there was a second of silence at the way Andy just stared watchfully.

"Hey, sorry," Devon said. He leaned in and kissed her, and she thought she tasted liquor.

"You been drinking?" she asked in a low voice.

He shook his head. "No, was just having a drink with coworkers when I got your reminder text, sorry."

From the way he said it and his expression, she realized he'd likely forgotten all about dinner. She was about to say something when Jeremy cut in.

"I may have created a problem for you," he said, and Tiffy rolled her eyes and brushed past him, shaking her head as if she knew something more.

"Oh, and that is?" Devon asked, dragging his gaze from Sara to Jeremy. She could see his confusion, how tired he was.

"It's nothing," Sara said. She knew Devon always worried about money. He was mister responsible and cheap. She looked again at the ring, fighting the urge to pull it off and see if it was only gold-plated, too. Would the metal soon leave a nasty brown mark?

It seemed Devon wasn't really listening to her, as he stared at Jeremy, who now shrugged.

"The ring," Jeremy said. "We were talking about it, and I may have over-spoken when I said it wasn't real."

"Ah, I see," Devon said before letting his gaze fall to her. "You don't like the ring."

She could see that this was becoming a problem. "I do like it," she said. "So how fake is it?"

Everyone was giving Devon all their attention, and she could feel how much he was in the hot seat, something else she knew he didn't like.

"Now you're making the guy feel bad," Jeremy said. "Seriously, I was there with Devon and helped him pick it out."

Sara only glanced her brother's way, knowing they were friends, still waiting for someone to say something.

"It didn't come from a crackerjack box, did it?" Tiffy jumped in, and the way she asked made everyone laugh.

"No," Devon said. "I assure you it set me back enough. The rock is a fake diamond that looks real, and the band is ten karats. The two diamonds on the side are real, though."

Sara lifted her hand, seeing the tiny specks. She didn't know a diamond could be that small.

"Where are they?" Elizabeth asked as she leaned in, staring at the ring.

"Maybe you need a magnifying glass to make them out. I can get one," Gabriel added.

Devon looked over to her brother, who was really putting the screws to him. There was laughing again, and she looked up at Devon, unsure of what she was seeing—unease, tiredness.

"It's fine, really," Sara said. "I love it. Besides, ring aside, Dad here is kind of in a mood…"

"You asked my daughter to marry you and you didn't even come and see me first," Andy cut in, all joking aside, still looking pissed off. "I want a word with you now."

She'd never seen her dad quite like this, and for that matter, she hadn't expected it. He jabbed his hand to Devon and stepped away from the sink, staring out of the kitchen.

"Uh, Dad, this really is between me and Devon," Sara said. "He asked me to marry him, and what we really should be talking about is a date and wedding plans. It's a moot point. It's done. I said yes…" She stopped talking as her father allowed his gaze to fall over her. Of course, it softened. She could convince him of anything. She'd always known just what to say.

He lifted his hand and touched her chin. "Not really, Sara," he said. "Don't forget, you're still my daughter."

She felt Devon's hand on her shoulder as he said, "Don't worry about it, Sara. Your dad's right. We'll talk."

She watched as he followed her dad out of the kitchen, and she took in her brothers, their wives, and her mom, who had wandered back in and was surveying the room.

"So what the hell is Dad saying to Devon?" Sara said, gesturing down the hall to his office, hearing the door close.

"Oh, he's likely scaring the ever-living shit out of him," Gabriel said, "saying he'd better see to it that your happiness comes before his and that he looks after you and doesn't hurt you. He's probably also making it clear that his life will be worth shit if he screws up in any way. That's about everything, right?"

Jeremy made an odd face. "Oh, and don't forget making sure that he spends the rest of his life not taking you for granted, and he'd better be financially together, because Dad won't be bailing him out, and he'd better be able to support you, and what the hell was he thinking, asking you to marry him before he talked to Dad first? That kind of fuck-up is likely going to haunt him forever. There's more, I'm sure."

Laura grinned as she reached for some of the celery Sara had cut and tossed a piece into her mouth.

"Seriously, that's kind of old school, isn't it?" Elizabeth said.

"Not really," Gabriel replied. "I asked your dad before I asked you."

Elizabeth looked shocked. "You're kidding, right? You asked my dad? Traditional values are not part of my family. You know that. Are you sure we're talking about…"

"Yup, your dad, Mr. Abercrombie, the very same. Elizabeth, it was just something my dad said before I proposed. He's your father, so I had to do it right. It doesn't matter if he doesn't expect it. It's a courtesy."

"Dad never said anything to me," Elizabeth said. They all knew that her family was dysfunctional in an entertaining way.

Gabriel shrugged and made a face as if it were no big deal, and Laura was still smiling.

Tiffy was staring at Jeremy, who wouldn't look her way. "I'm pretty sure you didn't ask my dad," she finally said, sounding so accusing.

"You're right," Jeremy said. "I didn't, but you'll be happy to know Dad sat me down and read me the riot act, saying I had better be a good husband, and I guarantee you he was a lot harder on me than Wayne ever would've been. If you'd like, I could go and talk to your dad now, apologize for not asking…"

Tiffy just shook her head, made a rude noise, and walked out of the kitchen.

"What? Tiffy, seriously…" Jeremy called out and started after her.

The two of them could go at it, but Sara knew they loved each other. Their history was filled with a lot of issues they had to continue to work out. She looked at her mom, who had said nothing. Laura chewed another piece of celery and then swallowed.

"This is ridiculous," Sara said. "We're already living together, and Dad was fine with that."

Laura leveled her with a look that had her realizing there was more to the situation. "No, Sara, you're wrong there. Your dad very much had a problem with you living with Devon, but they sat down together and talked, and I also said to him, living together is one thing, marriage is another. He agreed and eased up. You should know, he always expected to be asked as a courtesy."

"So Chelsea, too?" she said. She hadn't even considered Ric asking her dad for Chelsea's hand. Laura nodded, and Gabriel cleared his throat.

"Yeah, I remember that," he said. "Ric asked Dad, and Jeremy and I were there, too. Dad didn't go easy on him, but Ric didn't back down. I know Jeremy and I thought it was funny, the way Dad let him sweat, asked him a lot of hard questions, and then made it clear that if he broke Chelsea's heart or screwed around on her in any way, there wouldn't be a rock big enough for him to hide under."

Laura rested her hand on the counter. "Yup, your dad loves you all, but you all seem to forget something: It's not about being traditional and him giving his blessing. It's that the courtesy of asking says something about the kind of man someone is. It says he'll be able to look after his family. As your dad has said, if a man can't find the courage to look the father of the girl he plans to marry in the eye, then what kind of husband and father is he going to be?"

Sara didn't know what to say. She heard another vehicle pull in.

Her mom glanced out. "Okay, Zac's here. Elizabeth, set the table, and, Gabriel, take the roast out of the oven. As soon as your dad is done interrogating Devon and making him sit in the hot seat and squirm for a bit, we'll eat."

Before she could say anything else, she felt a hand on her shoulder.

Gabriel was shaking his head. "Stop worrying," he said. "Devon's fine. If he can't stand a little heat from Dad, then that tells you he's not the guy for you."

Devon didn't know any other person who could make him sweat like Sara's father could.

He didn't say anything as he watched Andy shrug out of his down vest, toss it over the back of his leather chair, and sit down, running his hand over his thick hair, a mix of dark and gray.

He was feeling the effects of the finger of scotch he'd been tossing back just as he'd gotten Sara's text. He was still kicking himself for forgetting about the family dinner and for telling Sara he'd been drinking with coworkers when in fact it had been just him and Kizzy.

He noted the closed door behind him and the fact that there wasn't another chair in the office. He could sense for a second how badly he'd messed up.

"Okay, should I start by saying I screwed up, badly?" he said, then waited and crossed his arms, feeling the dampness.

Part of him was still trying to make sense of what Jan Brown had said. She was tough and strategic and very good at what she did, but at the same time, he wondered if she really understood anything about him, his mother, and who they were.

Andy said nothing as he sat there and flicked those icy blue eyes up to him, his hands clasped over his stomach as he leaned back in the chair. It was unnerving, and Devon waited another second before realizing he wasn't going to say anything.

"I should have come to you before I asked Sara. I didn't think, and I'm sorry. I was distracted with my mother's case and with school…and I can tell by the way you're looking at me that you're not interested in my excuses, because there isn't one that's good enough. All I can say is I'm sorry, and although it may be a little late, I would like to ask your permission, or is it your blessing I'm supposed to ask for? It really seems old fashioned to me."

He took in the simmer of what seemed like anger in Andy's blue eyes. There were degrees, he knew, to Andy's anger and to his many moods. He didn't have a clue what the man was thinking.

"Just to be clear, it's nothing to do with being old fashioned. This is my daughter, and one day when you have children of your own, a daughter, you'll understand that there are expectations when some guy comes sniffing around. It's never too late, because I can still very much say no and make things very, very difficult for you. You know what, Devon? Doing what you did without coming out here and talking to me, man to man, face to face, borders on disrespect, and it kind of gives me an idea of how you'll treat my daughter. I'm not liking this."

The way he said it had him pausing, considering

what Sara would do if her dad said no. For a second, he thought that was what Andy was doing. He pulled in another breath. "Yes, sir, no disrespect intended. I would never do anything to hurt Sara. I love her. Sara and I are living together, and because of that I just assumed, logically…"

Andy's eyes flickered.

Devon knew he was managing only to dig himself deeper. Soon, there would be no way out. "I would like to apologize for not coming here first and would very much like your consent to marry Sara," he said, this time leaving out all the excuses. He'd learned firsthand in law school that excuses and ignorance were no defense for doing something stupid and breaking the law.

"You have a good head on your shoulders, Devon," Andy said. "I admire your loyalty and how hard you've worked on your mom's case, your dedication to law school, and the fact that you and Sara have been steady and together for a good few years. I like your character and your no-bullshit attitude. I'm pretty good at reading people, and I know you wouldn't ever treat Sara with disrespect intentionally, that you'd protect her. But I'm not sure, Devon, that you can give her everything."

What the fuck?

Devon froze, his chest tightening as his mind reeled. Had Andy just said no? He didn't like anyone questioning his loyalty, and it seemed that was exactly what Andy was doing, among other things.

"I can give her what I have," Devon said. "Nothing more. If you're talking about the ring, it was the best I could do without going broke and being irresponsible, as you so aptly put it. I have what I have."

Andy shook his head. "Forget the goddamn ring. I'm not talking about that, because you going into a mountain of debt for a piece of jewelry would be the kind of stupidity where I'd put my foot down and be sure you didn't marry my daughter. The ring is irrelevant. I want to know what your plans are. Where do you see yourself with my daughter five years down the road? Are you still living in that dump of an apartment? Is your brother still living with you? Is this something you plan to continue?"

Okay, so Andy wanted depth and plans. Now he really could feel himself sweat, because he didn't have that all figured out. "Well, as a matter of fact, I just mentioned to Sara that I want to move and find us someplace else, a safer place that doesn't have elevators breaking down and lights burning out. That's something I'm planning now, but it has to be within our budget. I'd like to buy her a house after I finish school, after I'm working full time, after I pass the bar and am earning a decent income and have paid off all my debts. You asked about my brother, too. Yes, he's there, and I don't know what to say about him. Do we always plan to have him living with us?" He didn't answer his own question, though, because Anton was his brother, his family, and he wasn't ready to completely cut him out.

Andy just nodded. He wasn't sure if he was saying the right thing or if Andy was testing him and was ready to tell him that no, he wasn't okay with him marrying Sara. This was a side of Andy he was unfamiliar with. He was a good man, and Devon had a load of respect for him, knowing well that Andy would seriously hurt him if he ever hurt his daughter.

"Go on, Devon," he said. "What about your

brother? You're looking for a new place, so does that mean your brother is moving with you? And then what about your mom when she gets out of prison? Have you thought about where she'll live?"

There it was. He wondered if this was the reason he was standing there, feeling very much as if he was being put through an inquisition. "So is that what this is about, my mom, the ex-con? You think I want to bring that around Sara?"

In fact, he'd refused to let Sara tag along with him to the prison every time he went to see his mom. There was just something about the one time he had taken her. He never wanted her there again. It had been hard, horrible, and dirty. He didn't want that touching Sara.

"No, Devon, this is about you. You want to marry my daughter, and you've yet to show me how you can be a good husband to her. I need to know your plans for a future. I'm not here to walk you through it. You need to show me not just with words but with actions, because your actions say everything about the kind of husband you'll be." He let it hang, and Devon had to fight the urge to jam his hands in his pockets.

"There's nothing I haven't done to put Sara first. I don't have all the answers…"

"No, you don't," Andy said. "There's something else, Devon. Having a drink or two is okay, but I can smell the booze on you from here. You forgot you were coming out for dinner, and it took a few texts from Sara to remind you. Yeah, I didn't miss that. A few drinks with coworkers? Priorities, Devon."

This time, Andy stood up and said nothing more. Devon was feeling very much as if he'd done something he shouldn't. He and Kizzy were just coworkers, friends, yet he'd said nothing about her. It was a secret that wasn't a secret.

"I'm sorry," he said. "I've got a lot on my plate."

Andy stopped beside him and rested a hand on his shoulder, eye to eye, and he wondered if the man could read his mind. It added to his unnerving feeling. "You do, and I'm not unsympathetic. In fact, I support you and respect what you're doing."

"I sense there's a big 'but' coming," he said.

Andy let his hand drop but didn't pull his gaze away. "You're right. There is. You've got too much going on, Devon. Yes, you're living with my daughter, but you have another year of law school, and you've put everything into freeing your mom from jail. You've paid your own way and haven't looked to anyone like they owe you something, and I admire that very much. It says a lot about you, but here it is. You have too much on your plate, and forgetting about my daughter because you're having drinks with another woman…"

"I'm not cheating on Sara! It was a work thing."

Andy made a face. "Guess there's my answer. Having drinks with a woman you work with came first, and Sara came second. You know that's a problem. So, tell you what. This engagement with my daughter, I think it's best that you put it on hold for now."

Was he serious? He wanted to laugh but thought better of it. Andy's expression was dark, dangerous, not a man to be crossed. "And for how long do you want me to put your daughter off? I've asked her already."

Andy rested his hand on his shoulder again. "Until you get everything sorted and figured out exactly where my daughter falls in your priorities. What won't be happening is you marrying my daughter while you're drowning in work, school, and life. Right now, she's having to fit into your schedule, your time, so when you have everything fixed in your life, then you and I can have this conversation again." He opened the door and stood there, gesturing toward Devon. "Well, let's go and have dinner with my family."

It wasn't lost on Devon that this was the first time Andy had used those words, "my family," as if he were just a guest. As he started walking down the hall, feeling his maybe future father-in-law behind him, he realized he was suddenly on the outside, looking in.

S he got home first, pulling into the back parking lot. Just the night before, Devon had displayed those overprotective instincts that she was missing right now, because where was he? Back at the office after leaving her parents' ranch, telling her to go on ahead because he had to go back for the files he'd forgotten.

Right, just like he forgot me.

She stepped out of the truck and clicked the fob to lock it, taking in the darkened parking lot and the door to the building, with the burnt-out bulb. So last night he'd been worried and today he was what, distracted?

At dinner, sitting around the table of roast beef and three salads—potatoes, slaw, and tossed—what had he done but eat in silence, saying less than he normally did? Even the quips he normally traded with her brothers had been nonexistent. Like, what the hell had happened with her dad?

"Hey, there, could you hold the door?"

She glanced over her shoulder, her key shoved in the lock, and spotted Anton, his hood up, jogging her way.

He was bigger than Devon, and his hoodie was over his head, which made him appear very much like a thug. She had to remind herself he was Devon's brother.

"So how was dinner with the parents?" he asked, his hand on the door frame.

She didn't know what to make of his question. "Great," she tossed out. "Just getting off work?"

He walked behind her down the concrete hallway to the door that led to the lobby. "Nah, went out for a burger. So, you and Devon. He popped the question, and I see you're sporting a ring, so I guess that answers that, not that I didn't know already. The walls are paper thin, and I can hear more than I want to when you two are talking. So when's the date?"

He reached around her to pull open the door to the lobby, letting her go first. It was gentlemanly, nothing she expected, not from Anton. She was still stuck on the fact that he could hear her and Devon in their bedroom, talking and doing what else? Then again, his room was beside theirs.

"He just asked me, Anton. Haven't set a date yet, but you'll be the first to know."

After they told her parents and her family, of course. She strode around the corner, seeing that the elevator was now working, and what did Anton do but reach around her and press the button for her?

"So where is Devon, anyway?" he said.

"He forgot something at the office, his files. I see the elevator's fixed." She gestured toward it.

The door slid open, and she stepped in. Anton pressed the button for five, and she noted the light was burnt out. "Yeah, talked with the super this morning," he said. "It's an old building, always something breaking down. You just have to be on his lazy ass, or he'll never do it." He made a weird noise, blowing out air the way people did when the silence turned awkward, and she could feel that he was just as on edge with her as she was with him. "So I wanted to clear the air with you, Sara, because all this back and forth between us is hurting my brother."

The elevator whirred and started climbing, and she took in Anton and the way he stared down at her. She wasn't sure what to make of the way he was watching her. There was just something about him that she couldn't figure out.

"Okay, clear the air about what?" she said, though she damn well knew what. She had to roll her shoulders, because the fact that Anton had dissed her over and over made it hard to forgive and play nice.

He let out a rough laugh. "Man, you really know how to grind a guy's gears and make things difficult."

She had to remind herself what Devon had said about his brother and their issues with each other. *Meet him halfway.* "Sorry," she said. "Okay, Anton, here it is. Devon and I are getting married, and you want to clear the air. I'm certainly open to that, because I know Devon wants both of us in his life, with no conflicts. I'm really tired of feeling as if I'm not wanted every time we're in the same room."

The elevator slowed and opened on their floor, and she hesitated and then stepped out, feeling his heat behind her as she continued on to their apartment. She seriously hoped that Devon meant what he'd said about finding them their own place. Maybe she should start the ball rolling.

"Great, because he's my little brother, and there isn't

anything I wouldn't do for him," Anton said. "You seem to make him happy—not sure why."

There it was, another slight. She had to roll her shoulders again, fighting the urge to look back at him. *Don't look. Don't look.* But she did it anyway as she reached the apartment, shoving the key in the lock and then stepping inside. He closed the door, and she slipped out of her coat. Inside, the galley kitchen was neat and tidy, something she hadn't expected.

"So is insulting me on the agenda? You're not sure why I make him happy, seriously? Anton, that really is a great start on fixing this between us."

He stopped in the kitchen and seemed to hesitate. "Look, Sara, I'm trying here. You think I don't know how you look down at me, how you think you're better than me, how you're trying to come between my brother and me? It's not right, Sara. I love my brother. He's all the family I have out here, and it's always been him and me. I've always looked after him and made sure he had everything I could give him, and he's busting his ass now to get our mom out of the joint. Are you going to come between her and Devon too? Is that your plan?"

The way he said it was like a slap to the face, and she realized he was serious. Had he really thought she was trying to drive a wedge between them? "I wouldn't do that, Anton," she said. "I know what you mean to Devon. I've never in any way tried to come between you two. In case you've forgotten, I live here with the two of you because Devon didn't want to leave. I also know Devon is doing everything he can to get your mom out, even after the public defender closed the case and told him to pack everything up. In fact, it was my dad who stepped in with his lawyer and…"

"Wait, wait, wait!" Anton shouted. "What the fuck do you mean, closed the case?"

Oh, shit. What had she done? She hadn't realized Devon hadn't talked to his brother. Her sharing this kind of information was exactly what Devon didn't like. They'd just talked about this. He was so private.

She could see by the way Anton was staring at her that he was waiting for her to answer. "I think you need to sit down and talk to Devon. I thought he told you, but it's kind of a moot point anyway. My dad stepped in and…"

"No, no, nope! You don't get to do that, not that. You don't get to dismiss me or blow me off. You tell me everything, right now," he said, cutting her off again, demanding. The way he spoke, the way he looked at her, the way he leaned in, it felt like a storm beginning to brew.

She said nothing, willing her tongue to move in a way that wasn't arrogant, as he'd just accused her of being.

"My brother seems to tell you more about my mother than he tells me," Anton continued. "I don't know how that sits with me. You're not family, you're not our blood, and you have no idea what Devon and I have had to do to survive. Our mother is our family, mine and Devon's. You're just a white girl from the right side of the tracks who's never had a difficult day in her privileged life. Evidently, you must be really fucking good in bed, 'cause Devon's got his head so far up your ass, doing things he'd never do if he was thinking clearly. You and your family have done everything you can—"

"Hey! What the fuck is going on here?"

The door slammed. She hadn't heard Devon come in.

"I can hear you two arguing all the way down the hall," he snapped. "I thought I was clear with both of you that I want this crap to end right fucking now, or did you not think I was serious?"

She'd never seen him this angry before. Anton just shook his head. She could see he was furious too, and she was fighting tears over the cruel words he'd just slapped her down with.

Angry, spiteful, mean. Those were the words that came to mind.

Devon stepped in and settled his briefcase on the table, so calm, as he let his gaze land on her and then Anton. "I'm tired," he said. "I've had a really shitty, hard day, so for fuck's sake, one of you start talking and just tell me what the hell the fucking problem is between the two of you."

She wasn't fooled by his calm stance, and he suddenly gave everything to his brother.

"You don't talk to Sara like that," he said. "That's a line you don't cross, Anton, no fucking way!" He sliced his hand through the air.

Anton crossed his arms and seemed to really settle into his stance. "You forget to tell me something, brother, like the fact that Mom's case was closed?"

"I told you it was reopened…" Sara started, but she stopped talking at the way Devon dragged his gaze over to her. The intensity, the anger was worse than she could have imagined.

"You told him," he said. His voice was low and accusatory, and she couldn't find the right words to explain.

"Not intentionally," she said. "I thought he knew."

Devon actually groaned, letting out a frustrated sigh, and she knew he was beyond furious. "It wasn't your place to tell Anton, Sara." He shook his head.

Her chest ached, and she swallowed, waiting for him to say something else, not knowing what to say to fix this.

Devon slid his gaze back over to his brother and didn't look her way when he said, "Sara, can you give us a minute? I need to talk to Anton."

It was a dismissal. It hurt, and she ached, because it was the same as him saying he didn't trust her.

"Sure," was all she said, and she backed away and took in the front door, their bedroom, and the ring he had given her, still on her finger, yet everything seemed far from settled. She listened to the silence, knowing they were waiting, so she walked to the door, pulled on her coat, and lifted her purse.

"I'll give you two some time," she said, and then she pulled open the door and stepped out into the hall, feeling empty and hurt, wondering where to go, what to do. Was this what she was in for with Devon, a life filled with conflict, a family that might just never accept her?

CHAPTER

Eleven

He heard the door close and knew Sara was hurt. It had been written all over her face. At the same time, he was furious, because she just didn't seem to get that his business, when they talked, was between them.

The last thing he wanted was her walking out that door, but how would he ever get her to understand that trust was everything, and it started with everything they shared? It was just one of those unspoken understandings. His business was personal, private, confidential. What didn't she understand? He shouldn't have had to tell her not to talk, not to share, not to discuss what they talked about. Private was private, especially between a man and his soon-to-be wife. So why was it that she kept opening her mouth?

"Is Mom's case open or closed? Come on, Devon," Anton said.

Devon heard him, but he was still smarting over everything from his day and from walking in and having to play referee between his brother and Sara, which was exactly what he hadn't wanted to do. "It's open now," he said.

His brother was shaking his head. "So it was closed, and you weren't going to tell me, but you told her?"

Okay, he was angry, and maybe he had a right to be.

"It was closed two days ago," Devon explained. "Then, yesterday, Sara's dad showed up with his lawyer, and she's taken it on pro bono. It's been reopened. End of story."

Anton just nodded, not pulling his gaze from Devon. "And you couldn't tell me? Seriously, like, what the fuck is up with you? This is Mom, our mother, yet you're telling her?" He jabbed his finger, pointing to the door as if Sara were still there.

Devon ran his hand over his face and picked up his cell phone. *Don't go far or make me worry,* he texted her, then put it back down on the table, seeing the three dots and waiting for her response.

Don't worry, just giving you space. Maybe we both need it.

He dragged his hand over his face again, pissed at her response and angry at her for not making this easier for him. He took another second to pull it together before trying to figure out the words to say to his brother, who was leaning against the sink, arms crossed, totally pissed.

"Look, Anton," he started. "Sara is my girl. We talk. She shouldn't have said anything, and that's totally, one hundred percent on me. I should have told you, so be mad at me. At the same time, I'm busting my ass to get Mom out, to fix this bullshit problem that she created. I'm sorry, but, Anton, you can't go around talking to Sara like that. You seriously called her a white girl and tossed out privilege, the right and wrong side of the tracks? I can't believe you threw the race card in her face. She doesn't deserve that. No one does, Anton. I guarantee you she doesn't see us that way, yet you're trying to make her into the bad guy, make her into a person who sees us as less and looks down her nose at us, when that couldn't be further from the truth."

Anton shrugged. "Well, she is a white girl, Devon— and you're just as black as me, yet you're trying to fit her into our world while you're trying to fit into hers. Ever since you moved her in here, you've changed. You seem to forget I'm your brother, we're blood…"

"And she's going to be my wife," Devon said. He didn't want to keep going around and around. After his talk with Andy, he didn't have a clue where the hell he stood, because he was still smarting over having been called out on everything, and he didn't want to admit that any of it was true. He just didn't get how everything was falling on him.

"You're really going to marry her?" Anton was shaking his head.

"We need to find our own place, Anton," he said. "This isn't working, and she's not leaving. I talked with you before I asked Sara to move in. Just yesterday, you said you remembered what you said."

His brother just stared at him. "I'm pretty sure I told you that you were crazy, that it would never work, but hey, who was I to stand in your way?"

"Yeah, you did, but I made it clear I wanted this thing with Sara to work and I needed you to get on board, to be nice to her, to not be a dick like you have been, Anton, because I can't deal with this shit between the two of you, and it seems to be escalating. Seeing the hurt on her face… You can be cruel when you're cornered, Anton, with some of the things you say. Sara is getting the brunt of it. This has to stop."

Anton actually lifted his hands. "Okay, I get it. I hear you. I'm sorry. She just pushes my buttons, being here, ordering me around. How do you think it makes me feel, having my home turned upside down by some girl you bring in here? Being told what I can and can't do, suddenly having to pick this up, do this…"

Devon lifted his hand and fisted it in the air, and his brother stopped talking. He must have known his frustration and the fact that he just couldn't deal with all this bullshit and the back and forth. "Look, if I have any chance of getting Mom out, I need to work, so you and Sara can either work things out and give me the peace I'm looking for so that I can put everything into Mom's case, or I can keep playing the peacekeeper and mediating this bullshit. Finding another place and having to cough up more for rent isn't ideal. I don't want to do it, Anton, but I will if you two can't work it out."

He thought back on what Andy had said. He really did feel as if he was all over the place.

His brother just lifted his hands in defense. "Just work on your case," he said. "Do what you need to do to get Mom out. I told you I'll make it right with Sara, I'll apologize. You're really going to marry her?"

He didn't want to answer again.

Anton just shook his head. "Well, just get Mom out. I guess I always thought you, me, and Mom would get something, our own place for the three of us. She's going to need us when she gets out."

Yeah, he understood that much. "I know she will," he said, "but one step at a time, Anton. Let's just get her out of jail, which won't be an easy feat. Then we'll figure out where she can go. Ideally, Sara and I'll move on, and Mom can move in here."

In the meantime, he still needed to get his head around what Jan Brown had said about his mom being broken. What would that mean for both him and Anton?

The work site was buzzing when she pulled up and parked behind one of two pickups, remembering that today was beam day. Gabriel had been a man down the day before, which had added to the tension and had him zeroing in on her, nagging more than usual about the budget and her need to constantly go way over. She didn't think she could take one more person coming down on her right now.

She pulled in another breath, shut her eyes, and leaned back, still smarting over the silence that had lingered between her and Devon since the night before, when he'd finally called her and told her to come back up. She'd been sitting in the lobby, leaning against the wall, taking in the door—which had been propped open again—and considering her options.

Someone knocked on her window, and she opened her eyes to see Gabriel, ball cap on and unshaven. He was really rocking that new beard. She opened her door.

"What, you didn't get enough sleep last night?" he

said. "You and Devon really got into celebrating and practicing for the honeymoon."

She stepped out and reached for her bag, and Gabriel held the door open for her. "Ha-ha, very funny. No, not much more than sleeping and work is going on at our place. Between his studying, working, and his mom's case, there's not much left for me. You'll be happy to know that I've given you one hundred percent of my attention in redoing all the designs." She shut the door and took in her brother, trying to figure out where his head was at. "I take it everyone showed today? Please let that beam be installed."

He tossed her an odd smile. "Everyone showed, so you're off the hook for having to listen to me complain. No more surprises, and everything went way easier than expected. Having said that, though, we kind of need to know about all the finishes and when everything is going to show up. Drywall is going in today, and you know once we start putting things back together, everyone needs to be here, and everyone starts showing up at the same time. I don't need to be paying contractors to stand around with their thumbs up their asses, so please tell me we're going to have everything on time."

"Well, not to worry. I've come up with a new design plan that just barely squeaks in on budget, and I think everyone will be happy with it. I placed the orders so that by the time you finish with the plumbing upgrades, electrical, and drywall, things should start showing up. I've already been assured everything is in stock, so there will be no delays. Do you want to see the new plans, or do you trust that I didn't screw something up?"

Gabriel raised a brow, giving her the oddest expression as they walked over to the driveway side by side, taking in the mud and the houses on either side. She knew the neighbors weren't that happy because of all the construction noise.

"Why do I get the feeling you're not talking about this project?" Gabriel said. "So how are things going with Devon and the wedding? You know I'm not the only one who didn't miss how quiet he was last night after his so-called talk with Dad. You didn't have to be in the room to know that Dad really put the screws to him."

She stared at Gabriel, wondering what he knew that she didn't. "So did you talk to Dad about what he said?" she asked, though she remembered that he, Elizabeth, and Shaunty had left earlier than she and Devon did.

"Didn't have to," he said. "I just know Dad. Could tell by his face, the way he looked at you, the way he was at dinner, and the way he seemed to hold Devon in his sights all night. Even Jeremy got it. I take it Devon didn't talk to you about it last night?"

She just shook her head. "Well, no, we haven't talked, and he hasn't said one word to me of what happened with Dad. We didn't get a chance, because we kind of got into it last night, and I'd say we're leaning more toward rethinking our entire relationship."

As soon as she said it, she lifted her hand and shook her head to stop him from saying anything. Maybe it was the surprise on her brother's face that had her realizing she was speaking out of turn again. She just couldn't win with Devon.

"You're having second thoughts?" he said.

She couldn't speak for a second. Behind Gabriel, through the open door to the house, the contractors were already working inside. She listened to the banging and everything about this construction site, which was like music to her ears. She loved it, tearing a home down and building it back up again. She loved everything about how this house was coming together, and she had given a piece of herself to this project. It wasn't lost on her how easy this was, even with all the complications and problems, as opposed to her relationship with Devon.

"Just wounded pride, I think," she replied. "I'm smarting a bit, really, after some of the things we said. Anton really came at me. Never before has he called me a white girl, and I really felt for the first time as if he was pointing out a racial problem with me and Devon."

The shock on Gabriel's face was priceless. "Seriously, and Devon knows?"

"He walked in on it. He was furious because of the yelling, the fighting. He asked me to give him space, him and his brother, so I did. I walked out the door with every intention of getting in my pickup and just driving, but then he texted me not to go far, so I just sat in the lobby as if I had to wait for him to tell me to come back. Like, how pathetic is that?"

Gabriel didn't say anything. The seconds ticked on.

"But I went back and saw him. Anton was gone. He studied, and I worked. I know he's angry at me because of his brother. I shouldn't even be telling you all this, because my mouth, my talking, is what seems to be getting me into a load of trouble with Devon. Anton and I have never got along. He tolerated me, but it seems so much like a war zone every night now."

She was tired, she realized, from all the back and forth, from going to bed alone every night. It seemed that Devon would study for hours at that dining table, which she had to constantly clear off. How he did it around his brother's video games was beyond her, and when he came to bed, she was sound asleep. They were like two ships passing in the night.

"How is your mouth getting you in trouble?"

She just looked at her brother, wondering if he and Elizabeth ever had the kind of arguments she and Devon did. It seemed he had no idea of the obstacles that seemed to be persistently in front of her and Devon.

"When Devon talks to me, he expects me not to share what we talk about," she said, "as if everything is confidential, and I get that. I get he has trust issues, but at the same time, I'm not sharing trade secrets. I mean, the other day, I was upset about his mom's ex-boyfriend, who is responsible for her being in jail and isn't doing the right thing, and Dad heard me venting to you, so he kind of rode in on his white horse and assigned his lawyer to the case. Instead of Devon being happy, because it actually was a good thing, and his mom's case is now reopened, he's angry because I talked. Then just last night, when Anton and I got into it again, I opened my mouth and let it slip that his mom's case had been reopened with Dad's lawyer's help. Even just saying it and listening to myself, I understand why Devon is angry, but at the same time, I can't help thinking he's overreacting."

Gabriel made a face, winced, and shifted. Then he shook his head and shrugged. "I don't know about that, Sara. In some ways, Devon's right."

What? Maybe he'd misunderstood what she was saying. "But if I hadn't said anything and Dad hadn't overheard…"

"Sara, the end result doesn't matter," Gabriel said.

"It wasn't your story to tell. I'd be angry too if Elizabeth was venting to her family about something I'd talked with her about. When you have a conversation with someone you love, there's an expectation that you won't talk. If he talks about and shares something personal, I mean, how would you feel if Devon was sharing your personal stuff with someone, your thoughts, your feelings, your problems, or something you didn't want anyone else to know? And his brother, I think you two have never really gotten along."

Not exactly the pep talk she wanted. "Wow, geez, why don't I come to you when I really need to be cheered up?" She hoped he'd picked up on her sarcasm, but all he did was give her an odd smile that really didn't reach his eyes. She took in his familiarity, the green of his eyes, the same shade as hers but a little different.

"Oh, Sara, Sara, Sara, my little sister, you really have a lot to learn," he said. "If you want this relationship to work and to have a future with Devon, you're going to have to work things out with him. If you don't want a future and you're questioning that now, then maybe you have your answer and you should break it off. If you're having these issues now, these problems, they're not going to go away if you get married. They'll only get bigger. And his brother…" Gabriel just shook his head and looked at her. "His brother is his family, Sara, just like us. How would you feel if one of us were constantly fighting with Devon?"

She knew she was frowning. "But you don't fight. You like Devon, and you all get along. I mean, Jeremy and Devon are friends, and Mom and Dad…"

Gabriel really looked at her as if he were making a point. "Yes, we gave Devon the benefit of the doubt for you, Sara, so how about cutting his brother some slack? The way I look at it, you moved into a space that Devon already shared with his brother. Maybe Anton is the one feeling as if he's being pushed out. I don't know what to tell you, but venting to me about your issues with Devon is likely only going to dig you in deeper with him. Would he be okay with you talking to me about your issues? Likely not. At the same time, you're my sister. You want out, you want to move home, just say the word, and Jeremy, Dad, and I will show up and move you out."

She said nothing and wondered why Gabriel was pushing so hard. "No, I'm not ready for that."

He nodded. "Good. Then why don't you figure out where you two stand?"

"Well, it's kind of hard, with the hours he works and the studying he does. There's not much time left for me."

"Really? You don't really need me to tell you what to do, do you? I mean, if he's that distracted, that busy, then why aren't you going to him? Take him dinner, surprise him at work. Do something, anything, because if you want this to work with him, you're going to have to figure it out."

Not what she'd expected from her brother. "So you're saying black lace and a trench coat?"

He lifted his hands and shook his head. "Too much information, Sara! Remember, you're still my sister. I don't want your sex life in my head—but if I was doing what Devon did, Elizabeth wouldn't just pull away. She'd surprise me with something creative." He rested his hand on her shoulder, maybe sensing she was about to ask him something more. "So, good talk. How about we get to work?"

She took in the house and then her brother. "So… can you give me an idea of the kind of creative surprise Elizabeth would give you?"

Gabriel shook his head. "Nope, I'm not discussing my sex life with my sister. Figure it out, but just a small word of advice." He started walking to the house and then turned to her. "Don't share it with me."

"My investigator is on it," Jan said. "I reached out to the prison warden about getting Darnell Watson to agree to see us. He has, but I'm thinking it's best that you don't go."

Devon took in Jan as she packed up her briefcase and gestured to him. Across the office, Kizzy was packing up for the day. He suddenly realized that the conference room, which everyone used, had been taken over for his mother's case.

"Why would you say that?" he said. "Of course I'm going—and how did you manage to convince him? I know I've tried, and so has Burton. Every time, he refused, which is why the case was closed. I have to be there to look him in the eye and make him tell the truth."

For a minute, based on her amused expression, he thought Jan was going to laugh. He took in her ultra-conservative outfit, a navy blue blouse and black dress pants with heels. Her earrings were thick gold, and they made him think of Sara's ring and the fact that he needed to figure out a lot of things with her. He didn't like the way things stood, and their relationship was just one more thing he had to deal with.

His clothes were clean today, and he knew it was Sara who had done his laundry, not the kind of thing he'd expected, considering all the angst around them right now, or rather, between his brother and her.

"First, Devon, the last thing we need, especially your mom, is you making this personal," Jan said. "For the record, my investigators can be persuasive. I can be persuasive. As you said, he refused your request, a very personal request from you. He knows what he's done, of course, but from what I've read, this guy isn't about doing the right thing. The last thing he wants is you shoving in his face what he needs to do to make things right. Honestly, he doesn't give a shit about you or your mom, or she wouldn't be where she is. My guess is that you don't have what he needs."

Jan was very deliberate in what she did. As she zipped up her briefcase, he couldn't help feeling pushed out of something he should have been handling.

"What do you mean, have what he needs? I should be there so he has to look me in the eye, to remind him of who I am, who my mother is, how he convinced her to take the fall for him, all the lives he's destroyed."

Jan gave a non-smile and lifted her gaze, jutting her chin to Kizzy, who had knocked on the open door before he could get his point across. "Kizzy is going with me," she said.

Kizzy stepped into the conference room, wearing a tan skirt and jacket, her dark hair pulled back in a tight bun. He took in her expression, as if she didn't know what to say and was worried about stepping on his toes.

"If it's all the same to you, I disagree," Devon said. "This is my case, my mother's case, and I want to be there and see this through to the end."

"And as I pointed out to you before, your mother could have been out by now," Jan said. "Look, Devon, this isn't about your ego. This is about getting your mom out. If you want to be effective on this case, you need to take the personal out of it and look at it objectively, and right now, I don't think you can. You make mistakes, otherwise. What you can do is go and pay a visit to your mom and get her to sign over the new counsel agreement, which will save me time and help us wrap this up soon.

"I'm hoping to get the motion before Judge Kluitz," she continued. "He's liberal, and we have a better chance of getting him to hear our motion, but that's only if we can get Darnell to come clean. To make my point again, Darnell isn't going to suddenly see the victims he's left in his wake and want to do the right thing. He's a hardened criminal, and as you said, this is personal with him. We don't need to be shoving it in his face so he refuses to cooperate. Right now, he has no incentive to come clean other than to be a good guy, and I don't need to point out to you that he isn't a good guy.

"Darnell has a long list of priors—guns, drugs, assault—and a history of dragging women into his world, your mom and others. The only thing he's concerned with is what's good for him, what can save his skin, and right now, because he's sitting in a cell and never getting out, we've got something to work with." She lifted her briefcase off the table and reached for her coat, which was resting over one of the wooden chairs. "You should get Kizzy up to speed, and then you should go and see your mom tomorrow, get her to sign the agreement, talk to her."

He was still stuck on what she'd said about Darnell saving his own skin. "What do you mean about working something out with Darnell?"

Jan was already packed up and ready to go. She turned to Kizzy. "You'll explain it to him," she said. "Listen, I have to go. I have to be in court in the morning. This isn't my only case, so Kizzy will get you up to speed. Then I need to depose your mom. We have a lot of balls in motion. Just remember that because your mom lied to get herself in there and refuses to lie now to a parole board to get herself out, the only chance we have is total exoneration. Considering all the strikes against her before she went in, I need you to get on board. Getting a case reopened for any reason is a huge uphill battle, and there are years of filed motions that go unheard." She lifted her wrist and looked at her watch. "Okay, I really have to go."

Then she walked out, and it was just him and Kizzy in a room full of files.

"I'm sorry, Devon," Kizzy said. "I know what you've put into this."

What was he supposed to say to that? This was one of the reasons he'd changed his entire focus and started law school. "It's why I'm here," he said. "Becoming a lawyer is because of my mother's case, and now I'm suddenly being shown the door. So when did you get pulled into this?"

Kizzy crossed her arms over her chest. "Just now. Burton called me into his office and said I was being assigned to help Jan and take the lead over from you. I tried to say no, but…"

He couldn't help feeling slighted. At the same time, this case had taken so much from him, his life and Sara's.

"I can see how pissed you are," Kizzy said. "Honestly, if I were in your shoes, I might not take it so well, either."

He just shook his head and laughed, but it wasn't funny, just absurd. "No, well, all I can say is I'm glad it's you and not one of the other clowns here."

She lifted a brow and said nothing for a second, then, "You want to get a drink and fill me in on the case? After all, you're the one who's been living this for so long, and our drink last night was short and sweet. We barely ordered when you had to run."

The reminder of the night before made him realize he still needed to talk to Sara, but here he was, still at work. His mom's case was turning his life upside down. He thought about what Andy had said, aware he was in no way okay with Devon marrying his daughter. He'd said Devon needed to fix his life, all this chaos—and this case was one of his biggest obstacles and had consumed so much of his time.

"Sure, let's go for a drink, and I'll let you pick my brain," Devon said. "Not sure what I can tell you about the case, but maybe I can give you something that will wrap this up sooner, get my mom out of jail."

Then he could get his life back and figure out his future with Sara.

Fourteen

Sara could've just gone home, but she couldn't get what Gabriel had said out of her mind. It wasn't even seven, and the sun was disappearing. She knew Devon would likely be at work still.

She strode down the sidewalk, seeing the sign and the stairs to the public defender's office. Of course, the lights were on inside, and she hesitated only a second, pulling out her phone before tucking it back in her purse. She hadn't seen his car parked out front.

She walked down the stairs and pulled on the industrial glass door, worried for a second that it could be locked, but she stepped inside and took in the half-empty office, looking around for him. She had been there only a few times before.

"Can I help you?" said a man with dark hair and glasses, a little overweight and about her height, in a baggy navy off-the-rack suit that appeared to be the wrong size.

"I'm looking for Devon," she said, wondering why

she didn't know any of the people who worked there. He didn't like talking about work.

The guy turned to the back of the room, to the clutter of empty desks. "Don't see him. Think he's gone already. Tyler, you seen Devon?"

The other guy, holding a coffee as he walked across the room, had dark hair and a white dress shirt and tie. "Yeah, he's out with Kizzy. They went over to the Hideout for a drink."

"And we weren't invited?" said the first guy. His wavy hair was a mess, a little on the longish side, and it looked as if he'd run his hands through it half a dozen times.

"Nah, don't feel like being the third wheel," Tyler said. "Besides, they didn't ask me."

She wanted to know who the hell Kizzy was and why the two of them were getting drinks alone.

"Did you have an appointment, or is there something I can help you with?" the first guy asked.

Sara just shook her head. "No, thought I'd drop by and surprise him, is all. Guess I should've sent him a text." She held up her hand and the ring, taking in the surprise he didn't try to hide.

"I didn't know Devon was getting married. You're his fiancée? Well, seems he's been holding out on us. Keeps his cards pretty close to his chest."

The guy named Tyler was leaning back in his chair, evidently interested in what she had to say, but it only made this situation more uncomfortable. Devon had time for a drink with a girl he worked with but not for her?

"You said he's at the Hideout?" she said. What was she doing?

"Yeah, the bar across the street and down on the corner," said the guy. "Do you want me to call him?"

"No, thanks. I'll head over there, surprise him," she said, and she pulled open the door and stepped out before they could say anything else.

She could call him herself, she realized. She had her keys in her hand and took in her parked pickup, feeling the anger, the hurt. She and Devon weren't on the same page.

She started walking down the block and spotted the bar, the words "third wheel" running through her head as she crossed the street. Two men walked into the bar ahead of her, tall and light haired, wearing suits and showing far too much interest in her. She looked away.

She didn't have to linger too long in the crowded bar before she saw Devon and a girl who had to be Kizzy, both laughing, smiling, totally into each other. She started across the bar, forcing a smile to her face.

Devon spotted her. His tie was loosened over the white shirt she'd washed. "Sara, hey!" he said. "Didn't know you were coming by. How'd you find me?" He leaned down and kissed her as she rested her hand on the bar table beside one of the empty stools. "Sara, this is Kizzy. Kizzy, Sara. Can I get you something to drink?"

She didn't wait for him to ask her to sit. "Whatever you're having," she said, pulling out a stool and taking in his glass of what she thought was whiskey. "Actually, on second thought, just a beer, a light draft, whatever's on tap."

He stepped away, leaving her with Kizzy.

"So you work with Devon?" she said. "You're a lawyer too?"

The woman smiled at her, watched her. It was awkward. "Yeah, have for a while. We're both second-year law students and started at the same time. He's one of the best." The way she said it, Sara felt the tension of the moment ramp up.

"He is," she replied.

"So, congratulations," Kizzy said, then shrugged and smiled.

Sara wasn't sure for a second what she was talking about. She was stuck on her confidence, on how much it had looked like she and Devon were together when she first walked in. She shook her head. "For?"

"Your engagement. Devon told me he was going to ask you. I saw the ring. I know he was worried about how you'd react to it." She flicked her hand to Sara's ring just as Devon appeared with a beer and slid it in front of her. He lifted his glass and took a swallow, and she squeezed her hands together, unable to take her eyes off him.

"React?" she said. Devon glanced between them, his expression questioning.

"Sorry, I may have misspoken about the ring," Kizzy said. "I think it's gorgeous, and it looks real enough to me."

Devon smiled, uncomfortable. She couldn't put her finger on his mood. She lifted the beer and took a swallow, wondering how it was that he seemed to have this other life with other people she knew nothing about, yet they knew about her.

"He showed you the ring before he asked me?" she said, still watching him.

Kizzy shrugged. "Just a woman's opinion. He was a little worried about how you'd react to it, if you'd like it

—but, as I told Devon, it's just a ring, and any woman with substance would love it and wouldn't want a fifty-thousand-dollar ring that would put him in a mountain of debt. You're getting a great guy, one a lot of women would love to have. So, in case I didn't tell you already, Devon, Sara, congrats! I hope you'll both be really happy."

She slid her gaze over to Kizzy, who downed the rest of her drink and then slid down off the stool.

"Okay, I'm going to go," Kizzy said. "I want to grab those files of your mom's and get started tonight." She reached into her purse.

"No, I've got it tonight, Kizzy," Devon said, lifting his hand. What was he doing? Sara just lifted her beer and took another swallow.

"I guess I did pay for yours last night, didn't I?" Kizzy said and laughed.

Sara hesitated. "You two were out last night?" she said. "So that's where you were when I texted you." She likely shouldn't have said anything. As she took in the two of them, the expression on Kizzy's face was priceless.

"And on that note, I'm going to go," Kizzy said. "It was great to meet you, Sara. Devon, thanks for the drink, and I'll see you tomorrow."

Then she was gone. Sara took in Devon as he lifted his drink and downed the rest. The expression on his face, which had been relaxed and teasing moments earlier, had turned hard, and that familiar tension returned.

"Don't make more of it than there is, Sara," he said. "It was just a drink after work, after a shitty day."

She knew she should let it go. "Never said it was a

big deal, Devon. It's just the way you said it, like it's such a secret, sneaking around. You were supposed to be out for dinner at the ranch to talk about the wedding, yet you were out having drinks with another woman." She lifted her beer and took another swallow before putting the glass down and slipping off the stool.

"You done here?" was all he said before he pulled his wallet from his back pocket and held up a twenty as the waitress came by. "For the drinks. Keep the change."

She started to the front door but felt his hand take hers and pull her around, back the other way to the back of the bar, where there was an exit sign over a door. He pushed, and she followed him down the dimly lit empty hallway, which she suspected led to the back alley.

"What are you doing, Devon? I'm parked out front of your office."

It happened so fast. He had her against the wall. His head lowered in a kiss that was both deep and possessive, animalistic. She could taste the whiskey. His hands slid over her ass and touched her breasts—rough, in public, in a way he'd never touched her before.

"**S**top," she said. She turned her head and broke the kiss just as he slid his hand under her shirt, lifting her bra and feeling her softness, the familiarity of her body, which could drive him crazy at times.

He was pressing her into the concrete wall, ready to strip her down and bury himself in her, in the tension, the touch, the chemistry that smoldered every time he was around her.

That one word brought everything to a close. He struggled, understanding what she meant, because all he wanted was her. He was ready for her now, but the word was like an icy splash of water.

It took his brain another second to really get what she meant. He didn't pull his hand away, instead sliding it around to feel the softness of her skin at the small of her back. "What?" he said, breathing heavy. He rested his forehead against hers, still touching her, his hand sliding up again, feeling everything familiar.

She hissed. Her hands were still looped over his

shoulders, running over his chest, touching him. He could feel how much she wanted him, but at the same time her hands pushed him and forced him to step back. "We can't do this here," she said.

He was no longer touching her. He felt possessive of her body, and for a second he really had to think about whether she'd said no. *Stop*, he told himself, taking in the dimly lit hallway and the back door.

A door around the corner opened, and someone was walking their way. It wasn't as private as he'd thought, and he realized what he'd almost done. He pulled his hand away, letting her pull at her shirt, righting herself, but he didn't step back.

"What's wrong with you?" she whispered. Her discomfort was written all over her face.

He heard a throat clear and turned his head to see a man—older, white, and watchful.

"You okay, ma'am?" the man said.

Was he serious? Devon found himself just staring, knowing that the look he was sending the man's way was murderous. He realized his hand was on Sara's arm, and she was still standing close. "You serious?" Devon snapped. "This is my fiancée. What the fuck business is this of yours?"

"I'm fine," Sara said, jumping in. He felt her hand on his chest, fisting in his shirt as if about to shake him or something. She flicked her hair, and the man nodded. After a few seconds of letting his gaze linger, he walked away.

Devon looked from her to the retreating guy, who obviously hadn't missed how gorgeous and sexy she was. A smarter man wouldn't have been so blatantly obvious in his appreciative look. Didn't he see Devon was right there?

Devon just shook his head, took her hand, and started to the backdoor exit, which went out to the alley. It was a route he was familiar with.

"Devon, seriously, what is it with you?" Sara said, pulling on his hand as he stepped outside into the dark.

He took in the emptiness of the night and then glanced at Sara, who looked so out of place. "You seriously missed that? He assumed you were in trouble. The way he looked at you for a second, I just knew he was seeing the color of my skin and thinking you couldn't be okay with someone like me. How long do you think it would've been before he dialed 911 and the cops were on their way? Still could be. Fuck, I don't like this shit!"

She made a face, and he let go of her hand, feeling frustrated and hurt. He wanted her so badly. He could feel too much. Everything was pulling him away from her.

"Really, Devon?" she said. "That is quite a reach. You keep bringing up race as if you believe everyone is living in another time when the color of your skin dictates who you are, who you can be with. Let me point out to you that it was you who had me up against a wall and nearly fucked me in the hallway of a bar as if I were a two-dollar whore. Anyone could've walked in and seen us. Is that real enough for you? That guy evidently picked up on what was going on, and it had nothing to do with the color of my skin or yours. If you were white, I guarantee you he would've said the same thing."

He got the bite of her temper, which she didn't show him often. At the same time, he wondered if she really believed what she'd said. "You don't see the world the same way I do, Sara," he replied. "You didn't grow up with nothing, having people looking down on you and expecting you to act some way because of who you are, having to constantly prove them wrong over and over. If it had been Kizzy against that wall instead of you, if the guy had stopped and said something at all, it would've been to tell us to get a room."

The expression on her face was as if he'd slapped her.

"I didn't mean it like that," he said.

"Really, so how did you mean it? Because it sounds to me as if there's something between you and Kizzy."

"Whoa, you're not serious. You're getting side-tracked." He actually laughed, and her eyes flickered with fire. He knew she wasn't about to listen to reason. "I only used the analogy to prove a point. Kizzy and I are friends. She's a coworker, that's it. She's working on my mother's case, taken it over. We were discussing it."

Bullshit! What the hell was he doing? He liked talking to Kizzy.

"You were having drinks together," Sara said. "You know what really pisses me off? I'm the one sitting in the background, waiting for you to toss a piece of yourself my way. Between law school and working in the public defender's office, you're always home late, and I've lost count of the number of nights I've gone to bed alone. I see more of your brother, who hates my guts, than I do you. Like, what the fuck are we doing? What are you doing?

"I can't believe I actually came here tonight to try to fix this between us, to do something that would fix this growing emptiness that I feel is changing everything. We're drifting further and further apart with this growing unrest, so much so that you're now sitting in a bar with another girl, as if you're under the impression that's okay in any way, and here I am, tossed to the side, waiting like some loyal mutt for some crumb of attention."

She lifted her hands in the air and made a rude noise. "You know what, Devon? You want to have a drink with Kizzy, or date her, or fuck her? You should do that. But consider this: I won't be sitting on the sidelines, waiting."

She pulled the ring off her finger and held it out to him, and there was so much in her eyes, so much anger, hurt, and betrayal. It punched him so hard in the gut that he thought he wheezed.

"What are you doing, Sara?"

All she did was hold the ring out to him, so expectantly, so final.

He couldn't lift his hand, so he just shook his head. "No," he said.

"Take it, Devon." She was determined, holding the ring right in front of his face.

"No, Sara! Is this where we are? Suddenly, after everything, you're making up scenarios of me cheating? I'm not." He just looked at her.

She slid her hand into his pocket, tucked the ring there, and then stepped back.

"Why?" was all he could get out, stunned and hurt that she could so easily just walk away.

"Maybe we've run our course. Maybe this is it," she said. "I don't know, Devon. What I do know is I'm not doing this anymore, coming second, having to realize that maybe you don't really love me the way I love you."

A tear slid down her cheek. She swiped it roughly as

she took a step back, then another, and turned and started walking away. Her boots clicked on the ground, and she looked so determined, her head held high. Then she was gone around the corner, and he was pretty sure Sara Friessen had just ended everything with him.

CHAPTER
Sixteen

There was something about the buzz and clang of the bars, a sound he didn't think he'd ever forget, the kind that settled in his bones. He realized it would haunt him forever. Just hearing it now after he signed his name in the book and followed the guard to the visiting room, it brought back what Jan had said, that his mother was now damaged goods.

He took in the concrete room and paced, seeing the table, the metal chairs, the paper and pens that the guards had okayed. When the door opened, he took her in: her jumpsuit, her long unruly hair, which was sticking up, and the smile on her face. She wasn't hand-cuffed, but the guard lingered behind her as she sat in the chair until Devon lifted his gaze and said, "Can you leave us, please? I'm her attorney."

And her son.

The door clanged shut, and the echo of metal on concrete was also something that didn't sit right in his soul.

"So am I getting a hearing? Will I ever get out?" his

mom said. She should be angry, but all he heard in her voice was hope, even though she was stuck in a hell he wouldn't have wished on anyone.

"I have a new lawyer on the case," he said. "I need you to sign that she can represent you." He slid the paper over to her, holding the pen out, not sitting down.

His mom looked at the paper, but he knew she hadn't read it as she signed her name where he pointed.

"You should really ask what you're signing," he said as he took in the eyes staring back at him, which were just like his.

"Why? You're my son. You tell me to sign, I will—or is there something more I should know?"

"You should really ask anyway. Question everything. Stop being so trusting," he said. Her trust was what had landed her in there.

"Would you betray me, have me sign something that would hurt me?"

Would he? He already had, he realized, when he'd pulled Jan Brown off the case so Burton could take over. It would haunt him forever. "Not intentionally," he replied.

She just shrugged, made a face. "Then you're making too much of nothing, boy. Tell me how you are. Tell me about the girl you're still with, Sara? Anton comes every visiting day. He tells me you're working hard on my case, and you're almost done studying to be a lawyer." She smiled then and clucked her tongue. "So proud of you, boy, our very own lawyer in the family."

She hadn't waited for him to say anything about Sara, and she hadn't said anything about how she was still in there because of him and his decisions. Maybe

Sara was right about that. Did he see the world against him when it really wasn't?

"Everyone's good," he said. "Mom, you should know that this lawyer is the one who started working on your case in the beginning, and I pulled her off. She's back on it. Do you want to know why?"

What was he doing?

His mother's gaze didn't pull away from his, but her brows knit together, and he could see her confusion. "What are you talking about, Devon? I'm not sure I understand what you're saying. Is she good?"

Of course she was. "Yes."

His mom nodded. "Then that's all I need to know… but it seems that there's something else. What is it?"

There was something about looking at his mother. He'd hated her for so long because she hadn't done the best she could for him and Anton. He'd been so angry and hurt that he hadn't seen how his ego and decisions had cost her time she could have had on the outside.

"You could've been out already," he finally said. "You're still in here because of me, because I pulled Jan off the case and brought it to the public defender, who didn't have the resources or pull she does. I let my ego take charge and decide what to do for you as if I could know what was best for your future, and because of that, you're still here."

Her expression said it all. She was confused, angry. "What are you talking about, Devon? You make no sense. You're becoming a lawyer to help me out, but you're trying to say that you're responsible for me being here?" She shook her head and lifted her hand as if she was having none of that. "Get it out of your head, Devon. I'm the only one responsible for me being here.

What are you thinking, boy? I was denied parole because I wouldn't speak the lie that put me here again. No, Devon, this isn't on you. This is all me."

"How can you say that? I just told you, you could already be out, but because of my decision to change lawyers, you're still here. You signed again because I asked you, and you don't know if I'm messing it up for you again." He was furious with himself. She was being way too nice, too reasonable, a different mother than the one he remembered from when he was a boy.

"Oh, Devon, if you were intentionally trying to screw me over, I don't think you'd be standing there, looking so damn guilty. At least I have you now. You're trying to get me out, and for that I thank you. Is that the reason you're so upset, or is there more?"

How could she not be furious? He still didn't get it. "Screwing up seems to be something I'm mastering as of late."

"What did you do?"

He pressed his hands to the back of the metal chair, picturing the ring Sara had shoved in his pocket and the empty bed he'd slept in at home. "I asked Sara to marry me," he said. He wasn't sure of the expression on his mom's face or the way she looked at him. "But Sara left me and gave the ring back last night."

"Because you asked her to marry you?"

He shook his head. "Because I'm an ass, selfish, all of the above and then some." He didn't know how to fix it or whether he should fix it.

"So this is why you look as if you're ready to kick your own ass. Don't remember ever having seen you so torn up."

"It's part of it," he said. "It seems I've been burning

both ends for so long I just took her for granted—trying to get you out, finishing law school, working. Then there's Anton. Seems I'm constantly playing referee between Sara and him, and I'm wondering if the color of our skin really does matter. Maybe I shouldn't be trying to fit into her world or fit her into mine. Maybe this is for the best." He paced the room, feeling his mom's eyes on him.

"Maybe it is if you believe it," she said. "She coming between you and Anton?"

He made a face. "No, she'd never do that. Sara is kind, thoughtful, but it seems she and Anton are like oil and water. Moving her into the apartment just added to the problem. I can see the way you're looking at me, like you think I should just let her go, because Anton is family, he's blood, and she's just a white girl."

His mom didn't smile or shrug. She just stared at him. "What does the color of her skin and yours have to do with all these problems you're having?" she said. "I don't care what color she is—white, brown, red, green… It's not about that. If you're trying to make something work that shouldn't, then look at the real reason. Your brother is a big boy, but I've told him every time he comes here to mind his manners with her. Do you love her?"

He hadn't expected this from his mom. He shrugged. "It's not that easy."

"I disagree," she said. "It is that easy, but it seems you're trying to make everything too difficult and taking on everyone's problems as if you have to fix them. I don't know her. I met her only the one time you brought her, and then never again."

He realized what his mom was getting at. "That

wasn't Sara. That was me. I wouldn't let her come again. I don't want her here, to see this. Every time I came out to see you, she wanted to come too, for me, for you."

His mom's eyes were watchful. She lowered her gaze to her hands, which were now on the table. "I see. Well, I guess there's your answer. Go make it right with her, Devon." She flicked her hand to the paper on the table. "Let the new lawyer handle things for me, and stop taking everything on as if it's your fault. You didn't answer me on whether you love her. Can you see your-self with her every day, growing old with her? Would it kill you to have to live without her?"

"It's too late," he said. "She gave the ring back."

This time his mom smiled and shook her head sadly, and he knew she was thinking of Anton's father, her true love. "Let me tell you what's too late," she said. "If she walked through the door of a convenience store and was shot and killed, that would be too late. This isn't too late. Go talk to her, apologize, make it right. But more than anything, Devon, be happy."

Seventeen

"Not going to work today?" Laura said as she walked into the kitchen. "Gabriel has called your cell phone at least a half dozen times, and your dad has paced that hallway and come in and out of the house to see if you're still here and if you'd like to enlighten us as to what's going on."

Sara sat at the kitchen table, the design plans for the job site spread out in front of her, staring but not really seeing what she was looking at. Laura rested a pot of tea on the table with a mug. For the two nights Sara had been there at the ranch, she hadn't pulled her aside or sat her down to find out what was going on. She'd expected it, once her family got past the shock of her walking in with a suitcase of her things.

Giving the ring back and walking away was the hardest thing she'd ever done.

She heard the door again and spotted her dad looking her way and then over to her mom, who she knew was keeping everyone away.

"Come on, Sara," Laura said. "I haven't said a word

to you since you walked through this door, saying it was over with Devon and that you gave the ring back. Neither have your dad or your brothers, but we're all wondering what happened. The only reason they aren't there in Devon's face, demanding some answers, is because I insisted they stay away."

Sara lifted her hands to her hair, which was an unbrushed mess, remembering the horror in everyone's eyes when she'd walked in on Jeremy, Tiffy, Zac, Brandon, and her mom and dad just finishing up dinner two nights earlier. She'd been embarrassed and hadn't wanted to talk.

She knew her dad was lingering again, and she heard his footsteps behind her in the kitchen. Her mom tossed him a glance over her shoulder, but she didn't move.

"So are you moving back in?" Laura said. "You gave Devon his ring back and broke up with him because…"

"It'll never work," Sara said. "There are too many obstacles against us in Devon's mind, and I can't keep dealing with his paranoia that we're from two different worlds. He seems to think that people are against us, out to get us, out to get him. Then with his mom's case and law school, I never have time with him. I'm just not interested in coming second. I'm supportive of him, but I never thought it would be this hard."

Her dad was now there, standing right behind her mom, and he didn't pull his gaze from her.

"Uh-huh, I see," Laura said. "Then it sounds to me as if you made the right decision, giving back the ring, moving back home, taking the easy way out."

What? She couldn't believe her mom had said that.

"Mom, you don't know what he did," she said, then bit her tongue, thinking of the world he'd come from. Having seen him with Kizzy, she was still stinging from the blinding jealousy, the realization of how good they looked together.

"Well, you haven't told us anything, Sara, so what are we to think?" Laura said. "He's done something, what?"

Andy slid his hand over Laura's shoulders as if to settle her, but Laura didn't pull her gaze from her. Her mom was tiny and strong, and she could read Sara better than anyone. At the same time, Sara didn't want to voice her worst fear—that Devon didn't really love her and could toss her away just like that.

"I'm waiting," Laura said. "You insisted on moving in with him even though your dad and I weren't really on board yet, and yes, he's up to his neck in getting his mom out of jail, trying to make things right, going to law school, working his ass off, but I know that every time he looks at you, he does it with so much love. He loves you. Marriage is hard, Sara, and there's no easy route. Are you looking for the easy way, not having to do the work? Do you still love him?"

Her dad still hadn't said anything, seeming more than happy to let her mom do all the talking.

"Of course I love him," Sara said, "and it's not about wanting easy. If I wanted easy, I wouldn't be with Devon…"

She heard footsteps outside on the steps, at the front door.

"Devon's here," Jeremy called out from the entryway. She hadn't even known he was home.

"Well, are you going to talk to him," Laura said, "or

would you like me to send your dad out and tell him to go and not come back?"

Why was her dad not saying anything? This was so unlike him.

She pushed back her chair and stood up. The baggy sweatpants she wore were comfortable but made her feel so unattractive. "No, as you've said, I'm a big girl. I'll talk to him." As she walked around the table, she felt her dad's hand on her arm, her shoulder.

"You sure?" he said. "I can show him my shotgun, tell him not to ever come back."

She knew he was joking, to a point—but at the same time, he wasn't. "Seriously…?" was all she said as she strode out of the kitchen on shaky legs.

When she reached the front door, Jeremy was already outside, and she could see him talking to Devon through the screen door. Devon looked better than she remembered. He was in blue jeans and a faded T-shirt, with a jacket pulled overtop.

She pushed open the screen door and felt them both look her way. She wondered how bad she looked, considering she still needed to have a shower, brush her hair, and get dressed.

"I'll catch you later," was all Jeremy said. He touched Devon's arm and then strode away.

She let the screen door slap closed as she stepped out, sock footed on the wooden porch, feeling the cold and crossing the arms of her long-sleeved shirt. He said nothing for a second as she stood there, staring at him and all that handsomeness: his eyes, his face, his broad shoulders, and damn, that chest. He was the full package, and just seeing him now had made her feel the giant hole in her heart, which had ached from the minute she'd walked away from him in that back alley. It stung like salt in a wound, and she couldn't believe that was even possible.

"How're you doing?" he said.

She shrugged. "Been better."

He took a step closer and rested his foot at the bottom of the porch, but she couldn't pull her hands from where they were wrapped protectively around her chest. She tried to tell herself it was because of the cold.

"I'm sorry," he said, and she really looked at him.

"For what, Devon?"

"For taking you for granted."

She hadn't expected that, and she wondered if her shock showed on her face. He didn't step back but instead took another step up, and then another, until he was standing right in front of her, so close that she could feel his heat, could touch him if she got up the courage to reach out to him.

"I love you, Sara," he said, "and you're right. I do make things harder at times than they need to be, but at the same time, that's who I am. I've seen things, done things, and I can't promise to be the perfect guy for you."

"I'm not looking for perfect, Devon, but I don't want to ever come second again. You were out with another woman."

She could hear the door squeak behind her. She didn't have to look back to know her dad was there, and her mom too, probably, from the way Devon shifted his gaze and looked past her.

"I had drinks with a coworker, a friend," he said. "It was a bad day. I didn't think how it would seem to you.

I'm sorry. There's nothing between us, and there never will be. She's not you."

She wanted to believe that, but she couldn't shake how it had felt to see Devon and Kizzy together, how right they had looked. "Do you have feelings for her?" she asked. There it was, the jealousy she hadn't realized she could feel. She didn't like feeling this way.

"Are you asking if I considered cheating on you, wanted to sleep with her, be with her, care about her?" He shook his head. "I love you. You're the only one I want to be with. Sara, when I think of my future and see where I am five years down the road, ten, twenty, I see you there. I don't see someone else with me. I don't want anyone else. I see you growing old with me, having kids with me, building a future, getting that house, traveling, seeing the world, doing stupid-ass things together, trying that new Chinese restaurant down on Fifth that you've been on me to take you out to, sleeping under the stars, moving to some new part of the world… It doesn't matter. The point I'm trying to make is that the only person I want to do all this with is you." He went down on his knee and reached for her hand. "Marry me, Sara. Be my wife and have this adventure with me in this life. Do it all with me, and forgive me when I screw up."

She glanced back and took in her mom and dad. Even Jeremy was standing at the round ring in the distance, watching. It was a spectacle, and she didn't know what to say. "I don't want to live with your brother anymore," was what finally came out.

"We won't," he said. He was still kneeling.

"I don't want to be taken for granted or feel as if I'm second, having to fight for a minute of your time and sharing you with anyone else, feeling like you have time for everyone else but me."

He shook his head again. "I can't promise I won't screw up and get busy, but I promise that I'll make time for you first. I'll spend a lifetime loving you, Sara."

She leaned her head back and shut her eyes. He stood up, but she still hadn't answered him.

"We'll get our own place," he said. "My mom's getting out. The lawyer came through. Jan and Kizzy got Darnell to confess. She didn't have to go to the judge, just worked it out with the DA. She'll be getting out soon, and she'll move in with Anton. That's all we've worked out." He was holding her hand now. "I can't afford much, but we'll look for a place tomorrow. No more case, just law school, just work—and you still haven't answered me."

She licked her lips and wondered why her dad hadn't said a word.

Devon reached into his pocket and pulled out the ring she'd given back. "Please, Sara, give me another chance."

The big rock really did look real, and something about it was so perfect for him, for her. "Okay," she said, and she lifted her hand.

"If it's all right with your dad," Devon said. "Sir, I would very much love to marry Sara, and I promise to be a great husband. I will put her first. I don't have much, but I will build a future with her and be there for her and work my ass off..." He still hadn't put the ring on her finger.

Sara found herself turning around. "Seriously, Dad?" she gestured to her finger.

Andy winked at her and then nodded. "Okay, it

seems that you're starting to get it," he said to Devon, letting his gaze linger between them. "Not before the spring, though—and, Devon, one more thing."

She wasn't sure what her dad was about to say, but she was sure her mom knew, by the way she looked up at him as if they were on the same page.

"Yes, sir?" Devon said.

Her dad gestured toward him with his chin. "Put the ring on her finger, and welcome to the family."

Devon didn't smile, just slipped the ring on, and her mom and dad walked back into the house. Jeremy lifted his hand and started into the barn.

Devon slid his arms around her lower back and pulled her closer. "I love you, Sara. You have no idea how worried I was you'd say no, that you'd tell me you'd had enough of my crap and couldn't do this anymore." He pressed a kiss to her lips and then pulled back.

"You really thought that?" she teased.

"Yeah, because this time I realized you were right about a lot of things. It took my mom to point out the obvious."

"Oh, now I'm curious."

He couldn't hide how he felt about her in the way he looked at her. It was everything she felt for him, too. "She loved Anton's father with everything in her," he explained. "He was the love of her life, just like you're mine, and she lost him. The fact is that just the thought of losing you was enough for me to realize I can't live without you. I don't want to have a life without you."

She just stayed in his arms, then rose up and pressed a kiss to his lips. "And you too, Devon. I can't imagine going through this life without you. We're really going to do this," she said.

He lifted his gaze over her head to the door, gesturing with his chin, and she looked back to see that no one was there. "Yeah, we are," he said. "So…your dad said not before the spring, so how about the first day of spring?"

She laughed. "Sure, Devon. That sounds absolutely perfect."

Epilogue

There was something about the concrete, the barred windows, the miles of wires, and the guards perched a hundred feet up, watching him now with a threat or a warning, protecting these walls and keeping the angry, horrible monsters locked away. Every one of the men inside this prison had been someone's child, with hopes and dreams of his own, and somewhere along the way, something had gone horribly wrong.

Everything about it was unfeeling, and as Andy Friessen stood outside in the cold, taking in the pale concrete against the gray sky, he knew nothing good could come from a place like this.

The wind picked up and rustled his neatly cut salt and pepper hair as he pulled at the collar of his black coat and shoved his hands in his pockets. He spotted a car in the distance and waited until the silver Malibu parked beside his rental SUV in the lot. He didn't move as the door opened and a woman he'd known for more than two decades stepped out.

Jan Brown had short dark hair and a round face, and she wore blue jeans and a tan wool coat. A dark-haired young woman stepped out the other side of the car, her wool coat frayed on the arms, her skirt wrinkled from sitting, and her boots scuffed.

"You been here long?" Jan said. She stood only five foot six, he thought, and he towered over her. The other woman was likely an inch shorter but a size or two bigger. She said nothing to him.

"Just got here," he replied. "So he's still willing to see us?"

Jan nodded, and he could see her breath as she exhaled. "As of last night, my last call to the warden. Let's remain cautiously optimistic and remember what the warden said: He can't be trusted, so don't tell him anything personal."

Andy stilled as he thought of his beautiful wife back home and his daughter Sara, who was the image of her. He thought of all his kids, who were just making their way in this world despite the roadblocks that seemed to be tossed in their paths. There was one thing about Andy: When cornered, he came out swinging, and right now, the man they were meeting had something he wanted.

"How long have we known each other?" Andy said.

There it was, the hint of a smile. Jan was the woman who made sure no one ever fucked with Andy, but she kept her personal life neatly tucked away. He'd heard rumors about a divorce long ago from a husband who'd picked her bank account clean, and now a new lover half her age.

"Long time," she said. "Well, let's do this. I have

other cases, and I want this wrapped up so I can move on."

He liked that about her, her straightforwardness. The other woman had fallen in beside Jan without a word, not commenting or needing to fill the awkward moment with frivolous small talk.

"Andy, this is Kizzy, a law student," Jan said, then turned to her. "So we're clear on your role, you won't talk to him, and I already filled you in on what the warden said about him. Any interest he sends your way, you won't engage. Give him nothing. Just sit there and do not answer."

"Yes, I understand," Kizzy replied. "So what if he doesn't sign the agreement or confess?"

The guard at the door buzzed them in. The concrete floor and walls were dark and dingy.

"You just sit there quietly," Jan said. "That's why I picked you to come, because of your ability to handle a delicate situation. He thinks he holds all the cards, and right now, unfortunately, he does. We go in there, and we need to all be on the same page so that he believes we have all the power. If he doesn't agree to our terms, then we'll walk, and he has nothing. This is it, all or nothing, and we have only one shot at this." She turned back to him. "This is for your daughter, Andy, and her fiancé. That's the only reason I'm here, working this."

There was another buzz as another barred door opened, and Andy waited for Jan and Kizzy to walk through and over to the square window.

A guard was on the other side, a light shining behind him. "Sign here, and leave your bags and coats," he instructed. "Cell phones, too. Anything you plan to take in will have to be searched first."

They handed all their personal effects over and signed in to the prison, and Andy took in the knitted black V-cut shirt Kizzy wore. She had a full bust (he suspected a D cup), and her skirt was tight at the hips. Her full lips were unsmiling.

He knew a few things from having read Jan's notes on her: She had the third-highest marks in her class, definitely competitive, and ass-kickingly good, but with a deadbeat leech of a boyfriend. Andy wondered how long it would take for Kizzy to figure that out.

What was it about strong, capable women that made them magnets for the losers of the world? He supposed Kizzy was simply following in Jan's footsteps in that regard. At the same time, he'd learned long ago that even people who could be relied on were not always heroes. Case in point, he definitely wasn't.

He took the clip-on visitor badge that the guard handed to him and clipped it to the pocket of his shirt, then looked up after he heard another buzz, seeing a different guard now, uniformed, wearing the same deadpan expression as the two before.

"We have only thirty minutes," Jan said, holding her briefcase again, first through the barred door.

Andy gestured for Kizzy, who hadn't pulled her gaze from him, to follow.

"I didn't expect you to be coming with us, Mr. Friessen," she said. She had fallen in beside him as Jan led the way, following the guard down another hallway, concrete and more bars ahead.

"Why wouldn't I?" was all he said.

She didn't shrug, just kept walking. There was something about the walls that seemed to ooze with death. Maybe that was why his heart was pounding, and he reminded himself to breathe past the feeling of panic in his chest. He wondered if this was what every man felt when he walked through these doors, many to never step outside again. At least he would be going home.

How many doors had they passed? There was an echo, the squeak of metal, the clang of keys, footsteps, voices, then shouting as another door was opened and closed. He figured they were inside the prison by now, and he and Kizzy followed Jan and the guard into a concrete room with a metal table, chairs, a light in the ceiling, and no window.

He listened to chains and the echo of footsteps, and then a man appeared, dark, tall, handcuffed, with prison tattoos on his forearms. Darnell Watson was big and strong, and Andy wondered if he could snap a man's neck if given a chance. He was put into the chair, and his dark eyes locked on to Andy's as a guard cuffed his ankle to the floor. Andy listened to the clang of the metal as the cuffs fell away.

Darnell rubbed his wrists, taking in Jan before his gaze landed on Kizzy and he made a sound of appreciation.

"I'll be just outside," the guard said. "Call if you need me."

Andy leaned against the concrete wall, looking down on this man, who was doing life.

"So is this pretty mama here for my conjugal visit?" Darnell said.

His tone had Andy stiffening, but Kizzy only flicked Darnell what he thought was a "Fuck you" expression. She kept it together. *Good girl!*

"Mr. Watson, we're here about Tiera Reed," Jan said. "You know, the woman who's doing life after taking the fall for you and your stolen guns. Right now, you could do the right thing and come clean. It will mean no more time is added to your sentence, and if you do, there's a deal that could even make your time easier."

Darnell laughed, deep in his chest. Andy took in the cut of the muscles in his forearms and the way he sat in the chair, shamelessly undressing Kizzy with his eyes. It took everything in him for Andy not to grab that piece of shit and make him mind himself, but Jan had already tossed him a look that told him to pull it together.

"Tiera who?" Darnell said.

Right, that was why they were there. Darnell wouldn't come clean for the crime he'd done, for grooming one woman after another, hiding behind them and taking cover. After all, it seemed he saw women as nothing but collateral damage.

"Are you finished being an asshole?" Jan said. "This is a time-sensitive offer, and the clock is ticking. Tiera Reed, young mother of two boys. Come on, you know what you did, telling her she'd get just a couple years and be out, yet the three-strike rule got her. She didn't hear from you again. You moved on, but the next woman was smarter. She wouldn't take the fall, and here you are."

He said nothing at first, then angled his head to Kizzy like a dog sniffing around a bitch in heat. "So who's she?"

"My assistant, another lawyer," Jan said. "So how about it, Darnell? Come clean and your life gets a lot easier."

The quiet echoed in the concrete room.

"It's the right thing to do," Kizzy said. She had

leaned forward, and even he could see the cleavage she didn't try to hide.

Darnell pulled back. "Not good enough," he said.

"So doing the right thing isn't for you?" Jan said. "I see that, but then, how many women have you talked into doing your bidding? They take the fall, carry the guns and the drugs, and you pick at them bit by bit, like a vulture."

He smiled. "So who's the angry white man in the corner who looks like he'd rather slit my throat than talk?" he said.

Andy didn't move and didn't uncross his arms.

"No one of importance," Jan said. "He's just here observing. Pretty sure you were offered something you'll never get otherwise."

Andy made a point of looking at his watch.

"Ten minutes is all you have," Jan continued, "and then we walk out that door and never come back, and you go back to that cell that you share with a man who cries himself to sleep every night, to the crazies who howl all the time. Bet you never expect to have a good night's sleep again. I can't imagine what that would be like, kind of like losing your mind bit by bit every day—and because this is a federal max in Pennsylvania, they don't allow conjugals. But what if you were transferred to a medium security, say, over in Washington, where it seems more like a country club?"

Darnell wasn't smiling anymore. Andy guessed he'd figured out who held all the power here.

"Say I do confess to something," he said. "How do I know that I'll get my transfer, that I'll get what you say? It seems to me that I have something you want, so let's do this. You get me the west coast, and get my sentence reduced."

There was just something about Darnell that told Andy the man wouldn't give them what they wanted. Of course, that would have been too easy.

Jan had her file open and wrote something down, then clicked her pen, closed the file, and tucked it into her briefcase. "Well, I guess we have our answer. I'd say that's time." She scraped back her chair, and Kizzy took her time getting up. Andy didn't miss Darnell's panic, his anger, the animalistic expression that said he could hurt them.

"Whoa, wait a second! What's going on?" he said. "You're not going. We're just negotiating. We're just getting started. Come on, sit back down."

But Jan had her hand on Kizzy's back and had moved her around the table, then tapped on the door. The chair scraped back, and Darnell was on his feet, but the chain clanged, and he couldn't move. The guard was there in an instant, slamming him down on the metal table. The sounds, the scent, the feeling of desperation —Andy wondered how many showers he would have to take to wash it all away.

"Don't go," Darnell called out. "What the fuck? I want a deal. You said you'd get me moved. I know her! Yes, I talked that stupid bitch into owning it. She was easy, like putty. You want to know everything? I'll tell you…"

He was still yelling, though the guard had him face down, his arms pinned back. Andy took in Jan's determined gaze, which flicked over to him.

"That will be fine then, Darnell," she said. "Guard, if you could sit him down?"

As Jan walked back around the table and the guard had Darnell sitting again, Andy appreciated how she could fool anyone into thinking she was soft and easy. He knew that he and Kizzy had been dismissed, and they started toward the door.

"So, Mr. Watson, just so we're clear," Jan continued behind them, "this in contingent on you coming clean on the crime, providing details that can be corroborated so that Tiera Reed, who is doing life for you, will then be free…"

"So that's it," Kizzy said as they walked back through the prison, led by another guard.

"Yeah, that's it," Andy replied. He stopped at the window with her, signing out, taking their things back. "I suppose this was a long way to come to just watch and listen," he added.

She stood before him as they waited for the guard to open the door. "With all due respect, Mr. Friessen, I'm not a fool," she replied. "I know you both used me because I'm his type, and that's the only reason I'm here."

For a second, he paused. He didn't know what to say, and he took in the guard ahead of them, who was expressionless but whose watchful eyes said he knew exactly what Andy and Jan had done.

He should've been ashamed, but instead he said, "I won't apologize. You're a smart woman. I owe you, so here is my gift to you: I want you to know that when you fly home with Jan tonight, you're going to walk in on your boyfriend with another woman in your bed, or you're going to check your bank account and find it's down another five hundred, and it's because you're that same strong, confident type that men like Darnell Watson find, groom, and take everything from."

Her face gave away nothing. When she went to answer, the guard interrupted them.

"He's right, ma'am," he said. "I see it every day. The signs are right there in front of you. You just need to open your eyes and see them."

Turn the page for a sneak peek of
HOW TO HEAL A HEART the next book in *THE
FRIESSENS*
Available in print, eBook and audio

How to Heal a Heart

NY Times & *USA Today* bestselling author Lorhainne Eckhart brings you a Friessen family novel about one man's choice to come to terms with a past that has secretly haunted him.

Gabriel Friessen can't shake his growing unrest at the idea that his seemingly perfect life is nothing but a lie he's spent a lifetime running away from.

Even though he loves his wife and step-daughter and has a family who loves him, he suspects that to move forward, he needs to close the door on his past—namely, on the man who is his father, his real father, who turned his back on his mother and left her alone and pregnant in what seemed to be another lifetime, before he was born.

Just getting on with things is no longer as easy as it has been all his life. Andy Friessen adopted him, gave him his name, raised him, and loved him, but part of Gabriel needs to face the man who turned his mother away. His mother has moved on, and his brothers and sisters would never understand, but Gabriel knows that to find the peace he needs, he must confront his biological father before he spirals any further into guilt and anger.

How to Heal a Heart

CHAPTER 1

"Shine the light over here," Gabriel said. He was on his back on the concrete slab in their crawlspace, feeling a rock or a pebble jabbing into his ass as he gripped the wrench, putting everything he had into loosening the pipe fitting. He could barely see in the dim light, feeling another drop of water hit his head just as the light flashed in his eyes, blinding him.

"Shit, Elizabeth! What the hell…" He shut his eyes and turned his head, the water dripping on his cheek now.

"I'm sorry," she said. "It's such a tight space. I'm doing the best I can."

The edge to her voice had him wanting to snap, but he forced himself to put the wrench down and rolled over, sliding down to where he could sit up.

"Seriously, Gabriel, how about hiring a professional to fix it?" she said. "You know a plumber."

He reached for the flashlight and took in the crawlspace around them. "I am a professional," he said, "and

I'm not spending money on a plumber when I can do it myself."

He didn't have to look over to Elizabeth to see her expression. Of course she was smarting, but then, he'd been an absolute ass as of late.

"Well, can it at least wait until the morning?" she said. "I mean, seriously, it's not as if this is a new leak that has to be fixed right now. It's been dripping for how long? I'm tired, you're tired."

"You know what? Go to bed, but I'm fixing this. Maybe that's the problem. There's far too much going on here that's been left for too long, so no, I'm not leaving it. I have a hell of a big day tomorrow. I need to be at the job site before sun-up, as all the tradespeople are showing up at the same time—flooring, finishing, electricians to install the lights… I need to be there so no one screws anything else up, or I'll have to go back and redo the job myself when I could have done it right to begin with."

Elizabeth flinched. Her long dark hair was pulled back in a messy bun, and she wore faded jeans with a hole in the knee and one of his blue hoodies, which was covered with paint splotches.

"So we're still there, are we?" she said. "Nobody can do anything right except you. Everyone is nothing but a screwup. You know, Gabriel, I'm doing my best, but there's days I wonder, from the things you say to me and others, whether you can hear yourself or have any idea how people are taking it. Why don't you tell me what's really going on?"

He took in the door to the crawlspace and then dragged his hand over his face. "Nothing is going on.

I'm sorry, I'm just…" Tired, pissed off, not sleeping—or was it that he could feel his once firm footing slipping in every area of his life?

She said nothing, just sat, crossing her legs on the concrete, in the grit and dirt, waiting patiently. Fuck, why did she have to be so damn patient?

He pulled in a breath, and even he could feel the frustration building. He wanted to snap, and he flicked his fingers through his hair. This time, he felt her hand on his arm, stopping him.

"Are you going to sit there all night and snap at me and at everyone else?" she said. "I mean, when my brother stopped by before dinner tonight, I don't remember you ever being so rude. Really, telling him we were about to eat dinner and asking how long he was planning on staying?"

Right, her family. He didn't have the patience for Marty, her wannabe biker brother, six foot two and three hundred plus pounds, dropping by anytime he wanted. He just wanted some peace and quiet. "I'll call him and apologize," Gabriel said, "but seriously, Elizabeth, just once I'd like to come home and not have to wonder if Ruby, Marty, or even your mom and dad are going to show up—and that ridiculous way they ring the doorbell, leaning on it over and over? Then I'm constantly having to throw on more food to feed your brother and sister, who it seems don't have lives of their own. They're always here."

Yeah, Elizabeth had the most dysfunctional family. They were entertaining, to say the least, but he was having a hard time dealing with them right now, wanting space and quiet and normal.

"Huh," she replied, and he didn't miss the edge. "So is this really about my family? You know Marty looks up to you, Gabriel, and you made him feel like absolute shit tonight, unwelcome. I can't remember you ever treating anyone in my family like that. Do you want me to tell my family not to come over, or is it that you want them to schedule an appointment? Is that what this is about?"

He kicked the wrench and shoved it over. The last thing he wanted was hard feelings, and this seemed to be heading to a place that could divide everyone. But what the hell did he want? How could he make her understand his own confusion?

"No, it's fine, but at the same time, how about some boundaries and space with your family? Do they have to be here every day?"

She made a face. "They're not here every day, Gabriel…" She lifted her hand when he went to interrupt her. "Ah, let me finish. Marty has been going through a rough patch, and he's been coming over here looking for some inspiration to get a handle on his diet. Did you know he had a panic attack? His doctor told him he had to clean up his diet and take off a lot of the excess weight. He sees how healthy you eat, and he's trying to do what you do."

He just stared at Elizabeth. He'd had no idea, and he wondered if the shock showed on his face. "I didn't know he had a panic attack. When? Why?"

Elizabeth inclined her head. "Last Thursday. He thought it was a heart attack and called me down. He was at a pawn shop, looking at a ring, wanting to pop the question to Bonnie."

Again, he wondered if his confusion showed. "Who's Bonnie?"

Elizabeth rolled her eyes. "You know, his girlfriend, the one he's been dating for eighteen months now?"

Right. Short, overweight, glasses, a few years older than Marty. How could he forget? He'd met her only once or maybe twice.

"Didn't know it was serious," he said. "How did I not know this? She's never with him when he comes by. A pawn shop for a ring, seriously?"

The way Elizabeth was staring at him, he realized how wrapped up he was in himself. She shrugged. "Well, considering how you made Marty feel tonight, it's a good thing she didn't come. Nevertheless, she works nights. And what can I say? Marty loves pawn shops." She paused. "But what happened with Marty tonight is kind of beside the point. You've been off for a while, and I've been pretty patient with you, beyond patient. Is this really about my family coming by? Because if it is, I'll tell them to stop just showing up if that would make you feel better."

Okay, now he felt like an absolute ass. Did her brother really look up to him? "No, I'm sorry. I'll call Marty tomorrow. I'll apologize. Is he really trying to clean up his diet?"

That was the way her entire family ate. Her father was the same, more than three hundred pounds, and her sister and mother were all about the TV dinners, the fast food. It was still a wonder to him how different Elizabeth was.

"Yup, he wants to still be around in ten, twenty years, to get married and have a future, to be more like you." She actually reached over and rested her hand on his jean-clad leg, rubbing. The way she looked at him, the intensity, had him feeling like he was really such a total and complete ass, so unworthy of her.

"Yeah, well, not sure picking me to look up to is such a wise move," he said, pulling back, feeling himself spiraling back into tiredness, disillusionment, everything he'd been drowning in as of late.

"Why would you say such a thing?" Elizabeth said. "Seriously, I have never heard you put yourself down—and for that matter, this mood of yours has been going on for a really long time, and I'm done with it. My brother looks up to you for the choices you've made, for the good, decent, and loving person you are, even though there are times like right now where I want to smack you silly. Look at everything you have, this place, your business. I thought you loved being a contractor, working for yourself, calling the shots. I mean, at least now you're not having to chase people around to get paid. Now you get to handle it all. You said this was your dream, and I've supported you. Good God, Gabriel, even Shaunty has seen how off you've been. You're distracted and moody, and we never know which Gabriel is going to walk through that door. I was starting to wonder if it was me."

Even though it was dark, with just the flashlight casting a soft beam, he didn't miss how her eyes seemed to glass over. She pressed her fingers to them and wiped.

"You thought it was you? No, Elizabeth, don't ever think that. Get that out of your head." He reached over and ran his hand over her arm and her cheek, feeling a tear he hadn't seen run down her face. She sniffed. What had he done?

"Then what is it, Gabriel? Because you're not sharing anything, and I'm not the only one who's been wondering what's going on with you. Even Sara said you snapped at her the other day. She called today and asked if everything was okay between the two of us. She said even your mom and dad and your brothers were wondering if our marriage was in trouble."

He could feel his jaw slacken as he racked his brain, trying to figure out how they could come up with such a ridiculous idea. He laughed and shook his head. "Geez, talk about reading into something. So my family's concerned for us, and what did you say to them?"

She shrugged. "It was just your sister, and she was worried. What was I supposed to say to her? Nothing, because I have no idea what's going on with you. You're a closed book, Gabriel, and when you don't want to let someone into your thoughts and feelings, they're not getting in. I know that, your family knows that. So if it's not me you're angry with, then who is it, Gabriel? I haven't pushed. I've given you space. Shaunty and I feel at times as if we're walking on eggshells around you. In case you forgot the part about us being married, I'm the one person you should be sharing with. For that matter, if it was me walking around, being moody and difficult and not sharing, I'm pretty sure you wouldn't give me the same space I've given you. Seriously, what was I supposed to think? I ask you something, you give me a one-word answer. We don't talk about our days, how Shaunty is doing in school. It's as if you've completely shut me out. You've stopped sharing anything…"

She lifted her hands, and he could feel the way the air was charged with emotion, anxiety, angst, and he was responsible for all of it.

"I want to find my father," he said.

She said nothing at first, staring at him as if he'd lost his mind. "Why?"

"That's why I said nothing, because of the look you're giving me now." He knew she didn't get it. "Because I want him to look me in the eye when I tell him he's a worthless piece of shit. No, scratch that." He gestured to himself. "What I really want is for him to look me in the eye and tell me he's sorry."

"Lorhainne Eckhart is one of my go to authors when I want a guaranteed good book. So many twists and turns, but also so much love and such a strong sense of family."

(LORA W., REVIEWER)

New York Times & USA Today bestseller Lorhainne Eckhart is best known for writing Raw Relatable Real Romance where "Morals and family are running themes." As one fan calls her, she is the "Queen of the family saga." (aherman) writing "the ups and downs of what goes on within a family but also with some suspense, angst and of course a bit of romance thrown in for good measure." Follow Lorhainne on Bookbub to receive alerts on New Releases and Sales and join her mailing list at LorhainneEckhart.com for her Monday Blog, all book news, giveaways and FREE reads. With over 120 books, audiobooks, and multiple series published and available at all, retailers now translated into six languages. She is a multiple recipient of the Readers' Favorite Award for Suspense and Romance, and lives in the Pacific Northwest on an island, is the mother of three, her oldest has autism and she is an advocate for never giving up on your dreams.

"Lorhainne Eckhart has this uncanny way of just hitting the spot every time with her books."

(CAROLINE L., REVIEWER)

The O'Connells: *The O'Connells of Livingston, Montana are not your typical family. A riveting collection of stories surrounding the ups and downs of what goes on within a family but also with some suspense, angst and of course a bit of romance thrown in for good measure. "I thought I loved the Friessens, but I absolutely adore the O'Connell's. Each and every book has different genres of stories, but the one thing in common is how she is able to wrap it around the family, which is the heart of each story." (C. Logue)*

The Friessens: *An emotional big family*

*romance series, the Friessen family siblings
find their relationships tested, lay their hearts
on the line, and discover lasting love!
"Lorhainne Eckhart is one of my go to
authors when I want a guaranteed good
book. So many twists and turns, but also so
much love and such a strong sense of family." (Lora W., Reviewer)*

The Parker Sisters: *The Parker Sisters are
a close-knit family, and like any other family
they have their ups and downs. Eckhart has
crafted another intense family drama…
"The character development is outstanding,
and the emotional investment is high…"
(Aherman, Reviewer)*

The McCabe Brothers: *Join the five
McCabe siblings on their journeys to the
dark and dangerous side of love! An intense,
exhilarating collection of romantic thrillers
you won't want to miss. — "Eckhart has a
new series that is definitely worth the read.
The queen of the family saga started this
series with a spin-off of her wildly
successful Friessen series." From a Readers'
Favorite award—winning author and
"queen of the family saga" (Aherman)*

Billy Jo McCabe Mystery: *The social
worker and the cop, an unlikely couple
drawn together on a small, secluded Pacific
Northwest island where nothing is as it*

seems. Protecting the innocent comes at a cost, and what seems to be a sleepy, quiet town is anything but.

Lorhainne loves to hear from her readers! You can connect with me at:

www.LorhainneEckhart.com
lorhainneeckhart.le@gmail.com

In the Silence
In the Charm
Unexpected Consequences
It Was Always You
The First Time I Saw You
Welcome to My Arms
Welcome to Boston
I'll Always Love You
Ground Rules
A Reason to Breathe
You Are My Everything
Anything For You
The Homecoming
Stay Away From My Daughter
The Bad Boy
A Place of Our Own
The Visitor
All About Devon
Long Past Dawn
How to Heal a Heart
Keep Me In Your Heart

The O'Connells
The Neighbor
The Third Call
The Secret Husband
The Quiet Day
The Commitment
The Missing Father
The Hometown Hero
Justice
The Family Secret
The Fallen O'Connell

The Return of the O'Connells
And The She Was Gone
The Stalker
The O'Connell Family Christmas
The Girl Next Door
Broken Promises
The Gatekeeper
The Hunted

The McCabe Brothers
Don't Stop Me (Vic)
Don't Catch Me (Chase)
Don't Run From Me (Aaron)
Don't Hide From Me (Luc)
Don't Leave Me (Claudia)
Out of Time

A Billy Jo McCabe Mystery
Nothing As it Seems
Hiding in Plain Sight
The Cold Case
The Trap
Above the Law
The Stranger at the Door
The Children
The Last Stand
The Charity
The Sacrifice

The Street Fighter
Finding Home
Finding Honor

The Wilde Brothers
The One (Joe and Margaret)
The Honeymoon, A Wilde Brothers Short
Friendly Fire (Logan and Julia)
Not Quite Married, A Wilde Brothers Short
A Matter of Trust (Ben and Carrie)
The Reckoning, A Wilde Brothers Christmas
Traded (Jake)
Unforgiven (Samuel)
The Holiday Bride

Married in Montana
His Promise
Love's Promise
A Promise of Forever

The Parker Sisters
Thrill of the Chase
The Dating Game
Play Hard to Get
What We Can't Have
Go Your Own Way
A June Wedding

Kate & Walker
One Night
Edge of Night
Last Night

Walk the Right Road Series
The Choice
Lost and Found
Merkaba

Bounty
Blown Away: The Final Chapter
He Came Back

The Saved Series
Saved
Vanished
Captured

Single Titles
Loving Christine

9 781998 775675